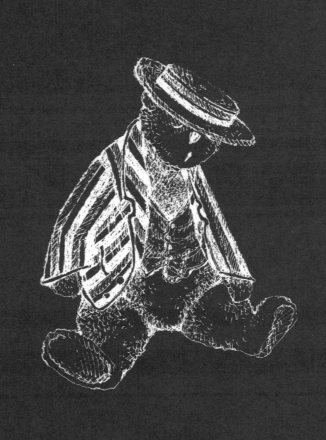

DRUMMOND

The Search for Sarah

For James and Tegan
S.F.O.

For My Mother
C.J.

Text copyright © Sally Farrell Odgers 1990
Illustrations copyright © Carol Jones 1990
First published by Walter McVitty Books, Australia
Printed in Hong Kong by South China Printing Company (1988) Limited

Library of Congress Cataloging-in-Publication Data

Odgers, Sally Farrell.
Drummond: the search for Sarah/Sally Farrell Odgers:
illustrated by Carol Jones.
p. cm.
Summary: A teddy bear, unexpectedly brought to life by Sarah and
Nicholas, begins a search for his original owner, a Sarah from an earlier time.
ISBN 0-8234-0851-5
[1. Teddy bears — Fiction. 2. Space and time — Fiction.]
I. Jones, Carol, ill.. II. Title.
P27.02375Dr 1990
[Fic] — dc20   90-55198   CIP   AC

SALLY FARRELL ODGERS

DRUMMOND

The Search for Sarah

Illustrated by Carol Jones

HOLIDAY HOUSE   NEW YORK

Contents

The bear's name was Drummond, and he was sitting on a chair in an empty room. He had been there for a long time now. He was waiting for his friend Sarah.

He stared at the doorhandle, which was too high for him to reach. Presently, he climbed down from the chair and levered himself up onto the window ledge, peering out through the panes. People came and went, but none of them was Sarah.

"Better face facts, Drummond old chap," said the bear to himself. "She's left you. And that's that."

New people came, but they had no use for the high attic room. Back on the chair, the bear sat gazing at the door. He sat and sat. He didn't see when the flowers came out in spring, nor when the leaves fell in the autumn. He ignored the winds that whined or whispered around the roof.

At last someone came, and picked up the bear, shook her head in puzzlement, and packed him away in the cupboard under the stairs.

And that was where he stayed, forgotten . . .

Chapter 1

The Bear

SARAH JORDAN and her brother Nicholas were perfectly ordinary people — until the day they met Drummond.

It really all began on the day that Mrs Harrington-Edwards decided to hold a Village Fair in the big garden of Hawthorne Hall, where she lived. Mrs Harrington-Edwards had bought the large old mansion some years before, when she needed somewhere to keep her horses. She was a tall, thin, leathery person, with a brown face, which was the result of being out in the weather so much.

"It's ridiculous, two old fogies like us rattling about in this great barn of a place," said Mrs Harrington-Edwards to her husband. "I'm going to have a real old-fashioned Village Fair. We can sell antique things like china teapots, patchwork quilts and old books and toys. Nothing modern."

"It'll be a lot of work," warned Mr Harrington-Edwards.

"Oh, I'll borrow Sarah and Nicholas," said his wife. "I'm sure they'd love to help."

And they did. Sarah and Nicholas found themselves spending the next holiday weekend with their great-aunt and uncle, at Hawthorne Hall, getting ready for the Fair.

They made lavender bags, and toffees and gingerbread men, and they went up the street to old Miss James', where they waited for half an hour while she finished crocheting the last woollen baby's blanket.

On the day of the Fair, Nicholas decided to test the sweets on the sweet stall. He was still very busy at it when his great-aunt found him. "I'll take over here, thank you," she said with a smile. "You go and help Sarah. She's fixing up the toy stall."

"But I haven't tested those yet," protested Nicholas, pointing to some toffees.

"Oh, I'll do that," said Mrs Harrington-Edwards, and she popped one into her mouth. "Off you go to Sarah."

His sister was setting out the old-fashioned toys on a table near the fence at the bottom of the garden. There were china dolls with mazes of fine cracks on their cheeks. There were smooth wooden trains, rubber balls, music boxes and even an old Noah's Ark. Then there were the teddy bears, some old and moth-eaten, with missing eyes and noses, and others still brown and fluffy, with bows around their necks.

"Sarah!" yelled Nicholas loudly, as he ran across the grass towards her.

"What's up?" she yelled back.

"Aunt Kath says I've got to help you!" bawled Nicholas, skidding to a stop in front of the toy stall.

"All right, all right, I heard you."

"Sarah? Where are you?"

"Right here, of course," said Sarah, lining up bags of marbles. "Don't go *on*, Nick!"

"I didn't say anything," exclaimed the surprised Nicholas.

"Sarah? Are you there, girl?"

The voice hadn't come from Nicholas at all. It was a deep, rusty sort of voice, and it sounded as if it hadn't been used for a very long time.

The children stared at one another, and then around the garden. There was no-one close by.

"Hurry up girl!" came the voice again. *"I've got a thing or two to say to you!"* It seemed to be coming from beneath the table.

"What...? Who...?" said Nicholas, still peering around them.

But Sarah knelt down and lifted the edge of the rug which was draped over the table.

"What is it?" asked Nicholas, keeping his ankles well out of the way in case whatever-it-was tried to grab him.

"It's only a teddy bear," said Sarah, and she pulled it out by one stumpy leg.

"*No, no no!*" scolded the voice. "*That is not the correct way at all!*"

Out in the sunlight, the bear blinked his small brown eyes anxiously under the brim of his straw hat. He was wearing a very smart-looking blazer, with stripes. "You're not Sarah!" he said in a smaller voice.

"Of course I am," stammered Sarah.

"Your name might be Sarah but you're not MY Sarah," complained the bear, before drooping lifelessly in the astonished girl's hands. She peered at it closely, and even shook it, but it said nothing more.

"How odd," said Sarah, holding the bear out to Nicholas.

Her brother turned it over. "I think it must be one of those bears with cassettes and batteries inside them," he said. "A boy in my class at school has got one. It must have got turned on by accident, or something."

"It can't be," said Sarah. "Aunt Kath said she was only collecting *old* toys — the sort she had when she was little. They didn't have talking bears in those days."

"He's probably clockwork then," said Nicholas.

"But there isn't anywhere to put a key," objected Sarah. "Put it down there beside the table. We'll ask Aunt Kath when she comes over."

Nicholas put the talking bear down and they finished unpacking the rest of the toys. But all the time the children kept wondering if

they had imagined it all.

Ten o'clock came, and people began arriving at the Fair, bright and colourful in summer dresses and shorts. The children were soon busy selling balls and marbles and wooden trains to their school friends. By lunch time it was quieter and families were settling down on the grass to open picnic hampers.

"How's it going, children?" asked Mrs Harrington-Edwards, coming over with a plate of sandwiches and two glasses of lemonade. She didn't wait for a reply but hurried away to serve sandwiches and drinks to all the friends she had persuaded to help on the stalls.

"Bother," said Sarah. "We should have asked her about that peculiar bear."

"I'll go and show her now," said Nicholas. "Where is it?"

"Here," said Sarah. But it wasn't. "Oh Nick! You must have sold it."

"Of course I didn't." said Nicholas indignantly.

"You must have."

13

"You probably sold it yourself," muttered Nicholas.

"I did not!"

"Well, *I* certainly didn't!"

"Well then, where is it?" asked Sarah.

"How should *I* know?" Nicholas sat down crossly to eat his lunch and sulk.

Sarah hunted through the piled-up toys, and looked into all the cardboard cartons. She lifted the rug and looked under the table, but there was no sign of the bear.

"Someone must have stolen it," she said at last. "Probably that Ronald McKeever. He was hanging about for long enough!"

"Perhaps it's run away," taunted Nicholas.

"Oh, don't be stupid!"

"Well, maybe he can walk, as well as talk," laughed Nicholas, as he returned to his sandwich.

And so Sarah looked around the stall again, and in all the boxes, in case they had made a mistake, but there was no yellow bear in an old-fashioned straw hat and blazer.

Suddenly, one of Mrs Harrington-Edwards' horses, which was standing by the fence watching the goings-on at the Fair, snorted and pricked up his ears. His neck arched as he peered at something odd on the ground.

"It's over there!" hissed Nicholas. "Look."

The children crept quickly over to the fence. The bear was crawling along very quietly, obviously trying to avoid being seen.

"It looks as if it's alive!" exclaimed Sarah.

She took a step forward, but a twig snapped beneath her foot. The bear froze, once more becoming an ordinary-looking teddy. Sarah scooped it up.

"The game's up," growled Nicholas, who was in the habit of watching too much television. "We've got you covered. You might as well give yourself up."

"Oh — all right," sighed the bear, and he came to life in Sarah's hands.

Chapter 2

The Bear's Story

"WHAT DO you want?" growled the bear.

"We want to know who you are," said Sarah.

"And *what* you are," added Nicholas.

"Well, put me down," growled the bear, "and then I might consider telling you."

"If you put him down, he'll run away again," warned Nicholas.

"Will you?" asked Sarah.

"Probably," said the bear.

A customer arrived to buy a china doll. When she had gone away, the bear hadn't moved. "This is no good," he said. "I never speak when adults are about."

"Well, we'll wait until later. . .if you promise not to run away," said Nicholas.

"No promises," said the bear shortly. "Just the word of a gentleman."

"But you're not a gentleman. You're only a teddy bear," objected Nicholas.

"There is no need to be offensive, young man," said the bear.

Since he refused to say anything more, Sarah put him gently into an empty carton, putting her sweater in first to make it more comfortable.

When the Fair ended at five o'clock, Mrs Harrington-Edwards came to help pack up the remaining toys. "Very well done, children," she said. "You've sold nearly everything! Hullo —

what's this?'' She bent down and lifted the bear out of the box. ''What a smart fellow!' she said, straightening the bear's straw hat. ''Did you forget to put him on the stall? Or has he been sold and is still waiting to be collected?''

''Not exactly,'' said Sarah uncomfortably.

''We found him under the table,'' explained Nicholas. ''We were going to ask you about it. Where did he come from, Aunt Kath? Do you know?''

''Goodness, how should I remember?'' asked their great-aunt. ''I've collected so many old toys from so many places over the past few weeks, there's no knowing what came from where.'' She looked thoughtfully at the bear. ''A nice one, isn't he?''

''We think he's lovely,'' said Sarah.

Nicholas hopped up and down with impatience.

Mrs Harrington-Edwards looked at them sharply. ''Tell you what I'll do,'' she said. ''How about I put a couple of dollars in the tin to make it square and you take him as a sort of present for all your work?''

''Oh, thank you Aunt Kath!'' said Sarah, and Nicholas puffed out his cheeks in a loud sigh of satisfaction.

* * *

The children stayed that night at their great-aunt's house. After supper they shut themselves in the upstairs bedroom with the bear between them on the bed.

''Well?'' said Sarah breathlessly.

''Well?'' said Nicholas, bouncing on his knees with excitement.

''Well what?'' said the creaky voice of the bear, as he sat up.

''Tell us!'' demanded Nicholas.

''Tell you what?''

''Everything!'' said the children together.

''Who you are...''

''How you can talk...''

''Everything!''

16

The bear settled himself on the quilt. "Well Drummond old bear," he muttered, "you sure know how to pick 'em, and no mistake!"

"Pick what?" demanded Nicholas, bouncing with impatience.

"Drat you boy! Stop that bumping about! You're like a ping-pong ball with the hiccups!"

"Who's Drummond?" said Sarah.

"I am," said the bear, haughtily.

"My name's Sarah," explained Sarah.

"I know," returned the bear. "That's how I got into this mess — hearing that boy call your name."

"How do you do?" said Sarah. She stuck out an awkward hand and, after a moment, the bear put his paw on her palm. "And this is my brother Nick."

"Pleased to meet you," said Drummond, not looking very pleased at all.

"What sort of mess are you in?" asked Sarah. "Maybe we can help!"

"Unlikely," said Drummond, sighing. "To put it bluntly, I've been deserted. Left in the lurch. Oh, I can see I'll have to start at the beginning. Settle down, do, and don't keep interrupting."

The children sat down quietly and stared at the bear, who seemed to be thinking deeply.

"Well, go on — how did you come to be on our stall?" prompted Nicholas. "Start there."

"No," said the bear.

"Well, tell us what you are then. A computer? Or just a clockwork teddy bear?"

Drummond shuddered. "I am a bear. Plain and simple."

"Not a real bear," said Nicholas.

"I'm as real as *you* are," exclaimed Drummond. "And don't you forget it!"

"No you're not," argued Nicholas. "You're only a toy. I'm a boy."

"I may have started out as a toy," said Drummond, "just as you started out as a baby. But you changed, didn't you? You're not still a baby."

Nicholas shrugged. "No, well...I grew up."

"Why?" asked the bear.

"They fed me on vegetables," said Nicholas gloomily. "Mum says that's what makes people grow."

"That might have made you grow," agreed Drummond, "but you grew up in your head too. How?"

Nicholas looked puzzled, but Sarah saw what the bear meant.

"We used to talk to him, and play with him," she said. "That's how he learnt to talk."

"Quite so," said Drummond. "But does he remember being a baby?"

Nicholas shook his head. "Not at all."

"And neither do I remember being a toy," said Drummond.

18

"The first thing I do remember was being with my friend Sarah and her father on a big ship. Sarah used to tell me all about how we were coming to this country, where we were going to live, all about her old home...all sorts of things. There isn't a great deal to do on a ship in the middle of the ocean, so Sarah and I spent a lot of time together. They were such wonderful days...just the two of us talking to each other, playing games, and just being great friends," said Drummond, finishing with a loud sigh.

"You mean that just because someone talked and played with you...you just...well...became a *real* bear?" asked the puzzled Sarah.

"Of course," replied the bear. "Why not?"

"Well, what happened next?" asked Nicholas. His eyes were like saucers as he listened intently to Drummond's story.

"Nothing," sighed Drummond. "They landed here, left me in a room, and never came back."

Sarah was horrified. "How awful...and mean!"

"Nevertheless, I am confident that my friend Sarah will be back for me very soon," said the bear stiffly. "I expect her at any moment."

"But what did you do when she left you all alone?" asked Nicholas.

"Naturally, I waited," said Drummond.

"But why didn't you go after them? I would have!"

"That, my boy, was impossible."

"He couldn't have gone out alone," put in Sarah quickly. "Somebody might have seen him!"

"That is so, young lady," agreed Drummond. "But I was unable to escape from the room, anyway. The doorhandle was too high. I couldn't reach it."

"So you just...waited!" concluded Nicholas.

"I *hibernated,*" said Drummond. "I only awoke today when I heard someone calling my friend Sarah's name...or so I thought. But I see I was mistaken. And now, if you will be so kind as to let me out of this house, I shall be on my way."

"But you *can't* just go away," said Nicholas.

"Thank you for your concern, my boy," said the bear nobly, "but I shall be quite safe."

"I didn't mean that," said Nicholas.

"Well, what *did* you mean then?"

"I meant you can't go away. You're ours! Aunt Kath said so!"

"Oh Nick, do be quiet!" said Sarah, glaring at her brother. She turned to the bear. "Of course we'll let you go, if you really want to," she said. "But wouldn't you like to stay? We might be able to help you find your friend Sarah."

"I suppose I *could* let you help," said Drummond, "if you're so set on it."

"Please stay," implored Sarah.

"Hm...well...so long as there's no more talk of *can't,*" huffed Drummond, with a disdainful glance at Nicholas. "What I choose to do is my own affair."

"I won't say it again."

"In that case, I shall accept your invitation," said Drummond grandly, "until such time as my friend comes to claim me."
He settled back against the pillow and carefully removed his hat.
"What a talking to I'll give that girl when I catch up with her!" he murmured. And then he fell asleep.

"He's a bit cranky, isn't he?" whispered Nicholas. "Perhaps that's why she left him!"

Sarah nodded. "I'm glad he's staying though," she said.
"I think he's nice!"

"Me too," agreed Nicholas.

Chapter 3

A Bear in a Bag

WHEN SARAH woke in the morning she pushed the hair out of her eyes and looked straight across at the chair where she had placed Drummond before going to sleep the night before.

As though sensing her gaze, the bear's eyes popped open. He sat up and stared sternly back at Sarah. "And what, may I ask, are you doing?"

"Lying in bed, of course!" said Sarah. "Why?"

"Why indeed! Just what I was wondering. I thought I was to be treated with consideration and respect while under your roof!"

Sarah was about to explain that she did not actually *live* at Hawthorne Hall but was only staying at her great-aunt's house overnight, when she heard Nicholas stirring in the next room. "I promised I wouldn't talk to you till Nick was here," she said.

"*I* made no such promise," said Drummond. "I don't hold with promises. 'Make 'em, break 'em or mistake 'em,' I always say. Just tell me what you mean by this outrage! Can't a bear have a bit of sleep without someone stealing his bed from under him?"

"But I couldn't have slept on the chair. I'm too big," said Sarah.

The bear turned his shoulder on her. "It's a wonder I didn't fall off during the night," he said peevishly. "Not that *you'd* have cared if I had. I want Sarah. My own Sarah, not you."

"We'll have to find her first," reminded Sarah.

The bear sagged, and was silent. How peculiar...he's turning

back into a toy! thought Sarah. I suppose this is what he meant when he said he hibernated. She touched the sleeve of his smart blazer, but it just felt like the arm of an ordinary toy.

There was a thump and a bang and Nicholas burst into the room. He had his shorts all twisted and there was one button left over on his shirt. "You said you'd wait for me!" he complained.

"I would have, but he kept on at me for making him spend the night on a chair."

"Hey bear!" hissed Nicholas. "Wake up! Mum will be here soon to take us home."

"I don't think he's going to talk any more now," said Sarah. "He's hibernating! How are we going to get him home?"

"Carry him, I suppose. If he keeps quiet, Mum won't even notice him."

"But what about Kate?"

"O-oh," said Nicholas. Kate was their young sister.

"Kate will talk," reminded Sarah.

Kate *always* talked. She talked about things she'd seen, things she'd heard and things she wasn't supposed to know about. She saw everything, heard everything and knew more than most people thought she knew.

The children shook their heads and agreed that they just had to keep Drummond hidden from the inquisitive eyes — and interfering hands — of Kate.

"If we can," said Nicholas, thinking of all the things he hadn't been able to hide from his little sister in the past.

"We could put him in my bag," said Sarah. "I wonder if he'd mind being shut up?"

"It would be for his own good," replied Nicholas. "I bet anyone'd rather be put in a bag than have Kate get at him."

Sarah looked doubtful.

"Remember what she did to Tumbledown Ted!" urged Nicholas. "She pulled his nose off and washed him in the bath. What if she did that to Drummond?"

Sarah shuddered.

And so they agreed to hide Drummond in the bag, between Sarah's nightdress and her spare tee shirt.

*　　*　　*

Their mother arrived to collect them after breakfast, hot and pink-faced. 'Phewwww!'' she said, flopping into a chair.

"Where's Kate?'' asked Nicholas, as he walked into the room.

Mum sat up with a jerk. "She was here a minute ago. Kate! Kate!'' she called.

There was a slithering crash, and a yell from the verandah. Nicholas and Sarah dashed out in time to see their small sister crawling out of a heap of crashed flower pots.

"I just climbed up on them,'' she said sweetly.

"Bring her in, children. Much damage?'' asked Mrs Harrington-Edwards.

"Only to the pots," said Nicholas.

"They'll sweep up," said their great-aunt. "Now run along and get your things."

Nicholas dashed off up the stairs, screeching round the landing like a racing car driver. Sarah had already collected her bag.

"Got him?" whispered Nick.

Sarah nodded and patted the bag. "He's still asleep," she replied.

They placed Sarah's bag on the front floor of the car, well out of Kate's reach. Nicholas had to get in the back but for once he didn't complain. He felt quietly important, doing his bit to keep Drummond a secret.

They were about half-way home when the bag suddenly began to buckle and heave between Sarah's feet. Alarmed, she looked down. The bag was wobbling about as if a small cat was inside, trying to escape. Sarah patted the bag reassuringly. It began to rock.

"What *are* you doing Sarah?" asked her mother.

"Just checking my bag," said Sarah.

"*Let me out!*" said a faint, but very annoyed, voice. "*At once, do you hear?*"

Sarah clasped the bag tightly between her ankles.

"Stop it, Nick," said Mum.

"*Let me out!*" insisted the voice.

"Ssh!" hissed Sarah.

"*Let me out!*"

"Nick!" said Sarah loudly and plainly. "Do be quiet! Can't you see Mum's trying to drive?"

"It wasn't *me*," began Nicholas. Then he realised what Sarah was trying to do. He just hoped Drummond understood her message too. Certainly, the bear didn't say any more, but the bag kept moving uneasily until Mrs Jordan switched off the engine and got out of the car.

"We're home!" Sarah announced, for the benefit of the bear, and scurried off round the back of the house.

25

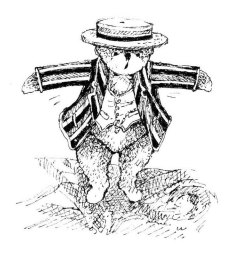

Chapter 4

A Bed for a Bear

SARAH KNEW that the back door would be unlocked. Her mother was like that. She'd often carefully lock the front of the house and not bother about the back.

By the time Mrs Jordan had juggled Kate and the shopping, then found the front door key, Sarah had already reached the room she shared with her little sister.

Nicholas darted along the passage and thumped on Sarah's door.

"Ni-i-ick!" complained Sarah.

"Let me in, then!"

Sarah opened the door just slightly and Nicholas slid through, wedging it shut with a chair on the inside — something he had often seen people do on television. There were two beds in the room. Sarah's had a blue cover with a ballerina pattern; Kate's was pink with flowers and butterflies, as well as a big brown stain where she had spilt a glass of chocolate milk. As Sarah was burrowing into her bag to find Drummond, his hat appeared over the rim. She put out a hand to help him out, but the bear swatted her crossly.

"*What* is the meaning of all this?" he demanded.

"All what?" asked Sarah.

"This!" the bear bellowed, as he landed on a pink and silver ballerina.

"We knew you wouldn't like it, but we had to get you here *somehow*," said Nicholas.

"Here? And where might *here* be?" enquired Drummond, smoothing his fur.

"It's *our* place!" said Nicholas. "Home. Where we live."

"We were only staying with Aunt Kath overnight, because of the Fair," explained Sarah.

"I see," said the bear. "And how did I get here?"

"In that bag," said Nicholas.

"I am well aware of that. But what made all that awful noise?"

It took some time before the children realised that Drummond was talking about the car. They could hardly believe that he had never been in one before. "I'll show you," offered Nicholas.

Not wanting to meet Kate or their mother, they left by the window. Sarah handed down Drummond, and then followed.

"There, that's our car," said Nicholas. "You *must* have seen one before!"

"Never," said Drummond, gazing at their car in the driveway.

"Well, he mightn't have, you know," said Sarah. "He was in a ship, remember? And then a house. That's all he remembers, so maybe he's never been in a car while he was...well...awake."

"So I arrived here in a car," said Drummond. "That still doesn't explain the *bag*."

"Oh, that was to keep you out of Kate's way," said Nicholas cheerfully. "If she'd got hold of you she'd probably have pulled your nose off."

Drummond quickly placed both paws over his nose, which was small and black. "What's a Kate?" he asked, in an alarmed, but muffled, voice.

"Our little sister," said Sarah.

"And she pulls the noses off *bears*?"

"Well, one bear, she did," said Nicholas.

"Poor old Tumbledown Ted. And after that..."

"*Stop, please! I don't want to hear!*" wailed Drummond. "Why didn't you just leave me where I was?"

"You'd have been stuck there for good," said Nicholas.

"Even that," muttered the bear, "would have been preferable to this Kate person. Just see that you keep her away from me."

They nodded, as he gingerly patted his nose.

"And that bag. No more of it, do you hear? Now, are you going to find my Sarah or aren't you?"

"If we can," said Sarah.

"You must," said Drummond firmly. "Since you have taken me away from that place, Hawthorne Hall, my Sarah — the real one — will not know where to look for me. So you must find her."

Sarah and Nick looked dismayed. They had no idea how many people lived in the coastal town of Hawthorne, but they didn't like their chances of finding one little girl, particularly as Drummond didn't know her last name. "Just Sarah," he had said grandly, when Sarah asked. "That's all I ever needed."

It proved more difficult to get back through the window than it had been to get out. Nicholas had only got his elbows on the sill when, after a quick look inside, he ducked and fell back into a lavender bush. "Kate!" he groaned.

"Where?" asked Sarah.

"In your room with Polly," said Nicholas. Polly was the dog.

"But didn't you wedge a chair against the door? What happened to that?"

Nicholas shrugged. "I did. But now it's upside down near the mirror. It'd take more than a chair to stop *her*."

They crept around and went into Nicholas' room instead. It had racing-car wallpaper, rather scuffed where he had raced his toy cars along with the printed ones.

"Drummond can live in here with me," said Nicholas. "You can't expect him to share your room with horrible Kate!"

"I'll sleep *there*," said Drummond, pointing a paw at the racing-car patterned quilt.

"But that's where *I* sleep," objected Nicholas. "I know, though!" He scrambled under the bed and pulled out a battered suitcase. "It's only got shoes and things in it," he said, spilling them out, "but it would make a perfect bed for a bear, with some old socks or something for padding."

"*Socks*?" said Drummond, glaring at Nicholas.

Sarah nudged her brother. "Don't worry, Drummond, I'll make a nice bed out of something of mine, just as soon as Kate gets out of my room. What was she doing in there, anyway, Nick?"

"Brushing Polly with your hairbrush," replied Nicholas with a grin.

"Oh, yuk!"

"*My* Sarah has lovely hair," said Drummond suddenly.

"Oh? It might help if we knew what she looked like. Tell us!"

"My Sarah," said Drummond firmly, "has long brown hair, in curls, and smiling blue eyes. She is a princess."

Chapter 5

Poor Drummond

OVER THE next few days Nicholas and Sarah learned a lot about Drummond's friend Sarah. In fact, they learned more than they really wanted to know. According to the bear, his Sarah was beautiful, witty, wise, well-mannered, clever, graceful, sweet-tempered, loving, neat, musical...and much more as well.

"She can't be *all* those things," said Nicholas. "No-one could!"

"You asked me what she was like," said Drummond. "So naturally I assumed you'd be interested in hearing the truth."

"She sounds like that awful doll of Kate's," muttered Nicholas.

"You mean Miss Prim?" said Sarah. "Yes, doesn't she!"

Nicholas climbed off Sarah's bed, opened the toy chest, and pulled out limp, stuffed rabbits, bits of jigsaw puzzle, plastic cars — and a big doll. This was dressed in a frilly print frock with an apron, white socks, black ankle-strap shoes and a large mobcap with *Miss Prim* on it. It simpered.

"There," she said to Drummond. "Does this look like your Sarah?"

Drummond gave the doll a scornful glance. "Certainly not," he said. "Put it away. I don't think much of *her*."

"Neither do I," agreed Nicholas, and he bundled Miss Prim back into the toy chest with the other things. Before he shut the lid, he turned to his sister with a peculiar expression on his face. "Sarah, you don't think this doll might be...sort of...*alive*, like Drummond, do you? Because if it is..."

"We shouldn't be putting it in a dark box," finished Sarah. "It'd be cruel."

"That's not exactly what I meant," shuddered Nicholas. "I just don't like the idea of *that* thing coming alive and walking about!"

"Never," said Drummond, from his seat on Sarah's pillow.

"How can you tell?"

"Easily. There's not a flicker, not a whisper. It's as dead as a..."

"Dolly!" said Nicholas and squawked with laughter.

"Oh, do be quiet Nick," said Sarah, giving him a shove. "Anyway, we were talking about Drummond's Sarah. If only we knew her last name!"

"I've never had call to use it," sniffed the bear.

"If this Sarah is so wonderful, how come she went off and left you?" interrupted Nicholas.

There was no answer.

"Well?" he demanded.

Drummond turned around slowly. He seemed to sag inside his elegant blazer. "Do you think I haven't asked myself that question nearly every day?" he mumbled sadly.

"Oh, poor Drummond," said Sarah, patting the bear's shoulder to comfort him and glaring at Nicholas.

"Sorry," mumbled Nicholas.

Drummond pushed Sarah away. "Sorry!", he snapped. "You don't understand in the least! How could you?"

"Understand what?" asked Nicholas.

"What it's like to be me!" cried Drummond. "My Sarah means everything to me! She brought me to life, she looked after me. I wouldn't *be* me if it wasn't for my Sarah! I'd just be like any other old stuffed toy...like that doll. And after all of that, Sarah left me. How could she have done it? That's what hurts me. If I only knew! There must have been a reason! So now do you see why I have to find her?"

Until then, the idea of searching for Drummond's friend had been a sort of game to Sarah and Nicholas...like hide-and-seek. It would be fun to be detectives and try to track down Drummond's friend, but nothing to worry too much about if they failed. After all, Drummond could always stay with them.

But now, hearing his sad tale, it was different.

"We'll find her for you, Drummond, I promise," said Sarah. "Just be patient, and stay with us a while longer."

33

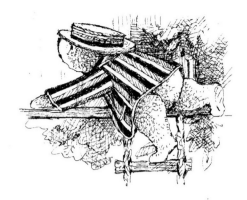

Chapter 6

Ideas

IT WAS easy to say they would find Drummond's Sarah, but now they had to think about how they would actually do it.

"Let's go out to the treehouse and think," suggested Nicholas.

Drummond refused to be carried. "I am perfectly capable of climbing a tree," he declared. "It is no more difficult than climbing a ladder, and that I have often done."

"Have you?" Nicholas asked. "When?"

"There was a ladder on the ship," he replied.

It took him some time to reach the treehouse, however, but he finally heaved himself up onto the platform.

"We haven't got much time," said Sarah uneasily. "School starts again next Tuesday."

"That's where we go to learn to read and write, and things like that," explained Nicholas.

The bear waved him aside. "I know all about school, thank you Nicholas. My Sarah has told me."

"Gosh, Nick," said Sarah excitedly, "why didn't we think of that sooner?"

Nicholas looked puzzled.

"She must go to school, mustn't she?" continued his sister. "What if she goes to *our* school?"

"I don't know any other people called Sarah," said Nicholas, "Do you?"

"No, but remember, she hasn't been here very long. Probably

she's just starting next week. How old is your Sarah, Drummond? As old as I am?''

"A little younger, I would judge," said Drummond. "But of course it is difficult to be sure. You are so very different."

"Well, if she's in either your class or mine, Sarah, we'll soon find out," said Nicholas. "You know how teachers always call out everyone's name. And if she's in another class, we'll just have to find out at lunch time. I only hope we know her when we see her."

"Of course *I* shall know her!" said Drummond frostily.

"Yes, Drummond dear, I'm sure you would," put in Sarah kindly. "But you won't be able to come to school with us."

"And why not?" demanded the bear.

"Nobody takes teddy bears to school," explained Sarah.

"Rebecca Anderson used to take hers for 'show-and-tell' when we were in kindergarten," Nicholas said.

"A sensible child," commented Drummond. He turned to Nicholas, who was perched on the edge of the treehouse, looking down at the lawn, where Polly the dog was bouncing and yapping at the foot of the tree. "*You* shall take me for this 'show-and-tell'," he ordered. "But not too much showing and NO telling!"

Nicholas shrugged. "All right. I suppose I could. But you'll have to keep quiet, and you'll have to travel in my bag. I'm not carrying you where everyone can see."

Drummond agreed to this with unexpected meekness. It made Sarah suspicious and she was just opening her mouth to say so when Polly began to bark some more and a chirping voice floated up. It was Kate. "Who are you talking to?" she demanded.

"Er. . . .Nick," said Sarah.

"Er. . . .Sarah," said Nicholas.

"I'm coming up, too," threatened Kate.

Drummond's paws instantly jerked towards his nose. He looked terrified.

"It's all right, she can't get you here," whispered Nicholas. But

Drummond was not convinced, and in the end Sarah had to climb down and entice Kate away before the frightened bear would even move.

Nicholas had been given a "sausage bag" for Christmas, and the children decided that Drummond could travel to school in that, along with all the felt pens, pads, clipboards, new books and other first-day-back-at-school things. Drummond didn't like the look of it at all, but he was determined to go, so into the bag it had to be.

"Any sacrifice or indignity is worthwhile if it leads me to my dear Sarah," he announced grandly.

"Just you remember that when I zip you into it next week," said Nicholas.

"I am tired," yawned Drummond. "Goodnight my friends."

"He's certainly cheered up," whispered Nicholas, as the bear climbed into his suitcase and fell asleep.

"Mmm," replied Sarah. "I just hope we can find his Sarah."

Chapter 7

Show-and-Tell

THE FIRST day back at school was a very trying one for Nicholas. As it was his first day in Miss Honey's class, his mother insisted on going with him. And that meant Kate had to come as well.

"This will be your desk, Nick," said Miss Honey. "You can unpack your things now, if you like."

But Nicholas couldn't do that while his mother and Kate were still there, because Drummond was on top of the books, just inside the bag.

Mrs Jordan lingered, admiring the bright posters around the walls.

"Nicholas..." said Miss Honey, who thought he was being too slow.

And then, to make things worse, Drummond woke up and tried to climb out of the bag. Nicholas had to put a clipboard on top to restrain the determined bear.

Finally, Mrs Jordan wandered towards the door, but Kate had begun to play with a box of counting beads, and wanted to stay. Her mother had to carry her away, and the angry wails echoing along the corridors made Nicholas wish that Kate was someone else's sister.

*   *   *

While Miss Honey was telling the children how much they were going to learn this year and how much they were going to enjoy it,

Nicholas suddenly remembered that he was supposed to be looking out for anyone new who could possibly be Drummond's Sarah. He peered around, and quickly spotted a girl he had never seem before. Could *she* be Drummond's Sarah? Nicholas wriggled with excitement. He'd have to make sure Drummond got a really close look. The girl did have brown hair but, though he craned his neck, he couldn't tell whether her eyes were blue or brown. She was looking shyly at the floor.

"Hey! Psst!" hissed Nicholas, just as Miss Honey stopped talking. The new girl seemed not to have heard him, but he soon realised that everyone else had.

"Yes, Nicholas?" said Miss Honey. The whole class turned to look at him. "Did you have something to tell us?"

Nicholas shook his head, wishing he was somewhere else.

"Are you sure?"

Nicholas felt that his ears were going red. Everyone was staring at him and he felt very embarrassed.

"All right everyone, let's have 'show-and-tell'," announced Miss Honey. "Who has something to show us?"

All around the room chidren were fetching the things they had brought to show. Nicholas followed, and lifted the clipboard off Drummond.

"Ssh!" whispered Nicholas, as Drummond batted at him with angry paws. "It's time for 'show-and-tell'."

"*Hat!*" whispered Drummond, and Nicholas pushed the bear's hat back away from his eyes. He was the last to sit down, so he settled Drummond as quickly as possible on his lap. Since the bear was awake, it was more like cuddling a live pet than a toy. Nicholas wondered uneasily if Drummond was going to be difficult.

All sorts of things were shown and told about, ranging from a green caterpillar in a jar to the latest remote-controlled model car with leopards painted on the doors. Nicholas peered at it enviously until it was his own turn. As Miss Honey nodded in his direction he got up, clutching Drummond to his shirt, and stepped up beside her.

"Well, well, what have we here?" exclaimed Miss Honey.

"His name is Drummond," replied Nicholas.

"Tell us all about him, while I hold him up so everyone can see."

Nicholas handed Drummond over, and held his breath. What if Miss Honey noticed he was alive? But apparently Miss Honey did not.

"Aunt Kath gave him to Sarah and me when we helped her at that Fair she had at her place in the holidays," Nicholas began. "We share him, but we have to keep him out of our little sister's way. She does terrible things to toys."

"I can imagine," murmured Miss Honey, who had seen Kate doing terrible things to the counting beads half an hour earlier.

"Very good," said Miss Honey, as she had said to everyone else who had brought something for "show-and-tell". But she seemed in no hurry to hand Drummond back. She was examining him carefully. Nicholas started to get worried. What if Drummond moved?

"He's quite unusual," said Miss Honey, tipping Drummond so that his paws were higher than his hat. "No label. Had your aunt had him for a long time?"

"I don't know," squeaked Nicholas. He could hardly bear to watch as Drummond hung upside down.

"Quite old-fashioned," remarked Miss Honey. "And beautifully made. This looks like a hand-sewn costume... and what's this?"

She was pulling gently at the silver chain which was looped across the front of Drummond's waistcoat. Nicholas blinked. He had thought the chain was just some way of keeping the blazer

done up. But Miss Honey kept on tugging, and after a moment one end of the chain came free.

"Ahhh!" sighed the children, goggling at the bear. For what lay in Miss Honey's palm was a round silver watch on the end of a chain.

"This is how gentlemen used to carry their watches before wristbands came into fashion early this century," she explained. "This is a very beautiful one. Nicholas and his sister are very lucky people." She handed Drummond back to Nicholas and then continued with "show-and-tell".

"Those children who brought us things to show can put them up on the ledge behind my desk for now," she said, when everyone had finished.

The children scrambled up from the mat, and headed for their desks. Nicholas wavered. He didn't want to put the bear up on the shelf. But Miss Honey was watching him. She seemed very interested in Drummond.

"I'll take you down at recess time," he whispered, as he settled the bear carefully between the caterpillar jar and the model car. "There's one new girl who might be your Sarah. The one in the red sweater."

Drummond remained silent.

The morning went slowly, and at recess time everyone seemed to be crowding round the shelf and looking at Drummond, stroking his fur, fingering his buttons, and peering at the little silver watch on the chain. Nicholas wanted to stop them, but when he tried to burrow through the mass of children, a boy named Ronald McKeever trod heavily on his toe and elbowed him in the arm — which might have been an accident, but probably wasn't.

And when Nicholas sneaked back into the classroom at half past twelve, Drummond was gone.

Chapter 8

Missing at School

NICHOLAS WAS alarmed.

He was sure Drummond had somehow got down from the shelf, and gone off round the school looking for his Sarah. By now Nicholas had discovered that the new girl in his classroom could not be the one they were looking for. Her name was Susan, and she had never been on a ship in her life.

And so Drummond had probably gone off searching on his own. At least two dreadful things could have happened to him. The first terrible possibility was that one of the teachers had caught him walking around, as no ordinary teddy bear ought to do. And the other terrible possibility was that one of the other children had done the same thing. Nick's head spun. He couldn't decide which would be worse.

If a teacher had captured Drummond, the bear might end up in a museum and be investigated to find out what made him the way he was.

If another child had him, then Drummond might be taken home to live with that child, and Sarah and Nicholas would probably never see him again.

Nicholas stared despairingly at the empty space between the caterpillar jar and the model car.

And then he began to have doubts. He knew that Drummond had trouble climbing up and down from beds and chairs, and the shelf was much higher off the ground than a chair. The more he

looked at the shelf, the less Nicholas believed that Drummond could have climbed down by himself. So he must have been helped down.

Nicholas stopped suddenly with his mouth open. Another thought had occurred to him. What if Drummond had been *stolen?*

"What's the matter with you, Nick Jordan?" asked bossy Angela James as she bounced into the classroom. "You're not supposed to be in here at lunch time."

"Neither are you," reminded Nicholas.

"I've got permission. So there," Angela boasted. Then she noticed the empty space where Drummond had been. She gasped. "Nick! Your teddy bear's gone!"

"I know that."

"It must have been stolen," announced Angela. "Miss Honey said it was probably worth a lot of money."

Nicholas didn't think Miss Honey had quite said that, but he nodded anyway.

"Do you want me to tell Miss Honey?" asked Angela. Nicholas shook his head, but she hardly noticed. "I bet I know who took it!" she continued. "I bet it was Ronald McKeever. I saw him looking at it."

"But everyone was looking at it," Nicholas reminded her.

"Not like Ronald though. Come on!" And she hauled Nicholas out into the playground and over to the climbing frames. Ronald

McKeever was hanging upside down from the log fort. His grubby knees were crossed over the rail, while his head and the tail of his shirt dangled in the breeze.

"Where's Nick's teddy?" demanded Angela.

Ronald dropped off the pole. "Ooh, I've broken my back!" he moaned, clutching his back and staggering round in circles. Then he took in what had been said. "How should I know?"

"Well, it's been stolen, and someone must have it," said Nicholas. His eyes darted around the playground, just in case he had been mistaken about Drummond's climbing skills. But there

was no stumpy yellow figure in sight.

"Well, it wasn't me," said Ronald as he punched Nicholas quite hard in the arm. It hurt, so Nicholas pushed him away. Ronald stumbled against the corner of the fort, and banged his ear.

"Ooh!" cried Angela disapprovingly, and dashed off to find the teacher on yard duty.

"Ronald McKeever and Nicholas Jordan are fighting, Mrs Davies," reported Angela. "Nicholas thinks Ronald took his teddy bear. It's worth a lot of money, the bear is. Miss Honey said so."

Mrs Davies sighed. "All right Angela, I'll look into it. There's no need for you to come with me, thank you."

She handed her cup of tea to Angela and marched off. Ronald was holding his ear with one hand and swinging at Nicholas with the other. Nicholas was swatting him back.

"All right, you two! What's going on?"

"He says I took his teddy bear. What'd I want with a mouldy old thing like that?"

Mrs Davies could deal with fighting, but stealing was a matter for the Principal, so she marched the two boys along to the office, and went to find their teacher, Miss Honey.

Mr Dowling frowned over the top of his glasses. "Fighting already! That's not a very good start to the year, is it?"

Nicholas glared at his toes. He wished he had never listened to busybody Angela. He wished he hadn't brought Drummond to school.

"Well, boys?" asked Mr Dowling.

"Sorry," muttered Nicholas.

"Ronald?"

Ronald McKeever made a noise which might have been an apology but which sounded more like a grunt.

"Stealing is a serious business," said Mr Dowling. "Let's hear your side of the story, Nicholas."

Just then Miss Honey arrived. "Excuse me, but might I ask what all this is about? Mrs Davies simply told me that two of my boys had been fighting and that you had asked to see me."

The Principal nodded. "I understand the boys were fighting over a certain teddy bear."

"Yours, I presume," said Miss Honey to Nicholas. "What about it?"

"I only asked him if he'd taken my bear," said Nicholas.

"I didn't do anything. He did it all," complained Ronald.

"Now Nicholas, what makes you think Ronald took your toy?" asked Mr Dowling.

"Er-hmm! Please excuse me for interrupting, Mr Dowling," said Miss Honey, "but it seems there has been an unfortunate mistake. I know for a fact that Ronald didn't take the bear."

The Principal looked baffled.

"Well, who did then?" burst out Nicholas.

"I'm afraid *I* did!" confessed Miss Honey.

*　　*　　*

As they walked home across St Luke's park, Nicholas told his sister all about his horrible day.

"Oh Nick," Sarah said, when she heard about the fight with Ronald.

"Oh Nick indeed!" echoed Drummond from the sausage bag.

"Well, how was I to know Miss Honey had taken you to the staffroom?" said Nicholas. "Teachers aren't supposed to have 'show-and-tell'."

Sarah looked puzzled. "Why did she?"

"She says she thought he was too valuable to leave on his own in the classroom, but I think she wanted to show him off to Mr Pearce. She said that he knows all about teddy bears."

"So what happened there?" Sarah asked Drummond as his head emerged above Nicholas' books in the sausage bag.

"You mean after I had been rudely pulled around, wedged under a clipboard, forced to share this bag with a messy school lunch, then put away on a high shelf without even a by-your-leave?"

Nicholas tried to explain that none of this was his fault, but the bear wasn't interested in anything but his own grievances. Sarah had to keep reminding him to keep his voice down whenever they passed other children going home.

"After these indignities, I was taken down and borne from the room," grumbled Drummond. "I was conveyed to another room where I was put on a low table with innumerable cups of coffee and sandwich plates. . . ."

"The staffroom," said Sarah.

"There I was handled by several people who all examined my eyes, my nose and my watch-chain. After some time of prodding and poking I was carried

back to the room with the shelf and returned to this bag.
I did not enjoy the experience in the least!''

"Neither did I," moaned Nicholas. "I've got a sore head and
Ronald McKeever hates me, and it's all your fault!"

"He doesn't mean it," said Sarah soothingly.

"Huh!" said Drummond, returning to the depths of the sausage
bag in disgust.

"What was that about a watch-chain?" Sarah wanted to know.
Nicholas' explanation lasted them almost all the way home.

"We didn't even find out about the other Sarah," complained
Nicholas. "So Drummond might as well have stayed home."

"At least we know she doesn't go to our school," said Sarah.

"Are you sure?" asked Drummond anxiously, as his head
reappeared over the rim of the bag.

"Quite sure," said Sarah. "I went to the secretary's office and asked Miss Wilson if any new girl called Sarah had started this year, and she said 'no'. I told her someone I knew had a friend called Sarah who might have been moving here."

"Oh!" Nicholas was impressed. "Then we didn't even need to take Drummond at all."

"The lady might have made a mistake," said Drummond.

Sarah said she hadn't. "Apart from the kindergarten children there were only three new enrolments this year, and two of those were boys. The other one was that girl in your class, Nick."

"Susan," and Nicholas.

"Oh," said Drummond sadly, and he said nothing more until they reached Nicholas' bedroom, where he instructed Nick to get rid of the messy banana peel with which he had been sharing the journey home.

Chapter 9

A Bear Alone

THE SUN had only just risen above the top end of the town when Drummond crept out of the house. He had decided to run away. It hadn't been too difficult to escape, as Nicholas had been careless with the door when he went to bed, and the kitchen door was fitted with a small hinged flap which was big enough to let Polly go in and out as she liked.

It was also big enough for Drummond.

The Jordan house was almost at the end of the street. At the very end, where the houses stopped, there was a belt of twisty trees and beyond that were the sand dunes which rolled away to the sea.

Drummond stood where the trees began and peered back at the white house he had just left. In one way he was sorry to be leaving Sarah and Nicholas. They had really been kind, and he knew they meant well. But, on the other hand, there was the dreaded Kate. How could he really relax when she was around? He wasn't frightened, exactly...but he badly wanted to keep his nose!

"And if you want a job done properly, Drummond old bear, you've got to stop relying on others and do it yourself," he said to the early morning.

The undergrowth barely rustled as the small, neat figure marched along. The birds sang their early morning songs just as if lone teddy bears passed that way every hour.

The trees thinned, and the wind began to hiss in the marram grass. Drummond climbed stolidly up one of the shifting dunes. It

was very hard work, and his paws sank into the cold, dry sand. He stumbled forward and continued on all four legs. This made climbing easier, but he could no longer see far in front because of the brim of his hat. At the top of the dune he raised his head as much as he could, and caught a glimpse of the damp, wave-ribbed beach away below. Then he started down the other side. And that was where he made his mistake. The seaward side of the dune was much steeper than the other, being cut and carved almost into an overhang by the wind. Drummond's paws slipped and slithered in the loose sand, and with a startled cry he began to fall, tumbling over and over, to land down at the foot of the dunes in a small avalanche of sand.

Drummond lay there for some time with his nose in the sand and his paws scrabbling for a hold on the soft surface. He could hear the hiss and hush of the waves, and the sound of the wind coming in from the sea. He remembered the smell of the salt air. Hadn't he and his Sarah leaned on the ship's rail and breathed in the very same scent? He could almost imagine he was there with her now. That sound he could hear — was it the slap of the waves against the sides of the ship? Drummond tried very hard to believe it was, but soon he could hear something else: a loud, regular panting, as if someone had been running for a long time. He shook the sand out of his eyes and tried to push back his hat at the same time. The sounds came closer.

It was a runner, out for an early morning jog along the beach.

Drummond froze into stillness, and hoped the runner wouldn't notice him. Then, just as he decided it was safe to clamber out of his sand nest, something wet touched his nose and an enormous face loomed down on a level with his own. The face had a moist black nose, floppy lop-ears, eager brown eyes and a huge mouthful of teeth and tongue. It was a dog.

Although Drummond was terrified of the dog, the dog was very interested indeed in Drummond. It had seen him move, which seemed to mean he was alive. But one or two deep sniffs convinced it that Drummond was neither dog nor cat nor rabbit. And he certainly didn't smell like a dead fish, which was what the dog might have expected to find washed up on the beach. It was perplexed, and it tried to turn him over with its nose.

Drummond did his best to roll up into a ball, and the dog scraped at his jacket with its front paws.

"G-go away!" said Drummond.

The dog backed off a few steps and whined. Drummond tried to climb backwards up the dune. The dog rushed forwards and pounced, playfully. This thing — whatever it was — seemed to want a game. And playing with a mysterious creature was much more entertaining than following its master on his daily run.

"Stop it!" cried Drummond, trying to burrow into the dune. "Get away!"

Unfortunately, this excited the dog more, and it began to frisk and bounce and whine, uttering shrill little yaps.

"No!" protested Drummond, as the dog tugged at his blazer with impatient teeth.

At first Drummond didn't hear the whistle. But the dog did. It raised its head, with the bear dangling from its jaws, and pricked its lop-ears as far as they would go. The whistle came again, loud and shrill. The dog barked once, dropping Drummond in a heap of scratchy marram grass. The whistle was repeated, from nearer at hand. And now Drummond knew what it was. He had heard Sarah and Nicholas calling for their dog Polly in the same way.

"Well go on — *go-go-go-* " he urged the dog. It seemed to waver, glancing over its shoulder.

"Rusty! Rusty! Here! Come out of that!" The runner came
closer, and he sounded at least as eager to get the dog away from
Drummond as Drummond was to see it go. A long stick began to
poke at the clump of grass where Drummond was cowering. "Back
Rusty!" The runner pulled the dog away by its collar, and leaned
cautiously closer. "Oh, it's only a dirty old toy. You *stupid* animal;
I thought you'd found a snake or something interesting! Come *on!*"
The dog was dragged away.

Drummond lay shaking, as the indignant choking yaps died
away in the distance. Then he rose carefully and shook himself to
get rid of the sand. "Dirty old toy indeed!" Drummond muttered.
"What stupidity!" But he was still shaking. The world was a
dangerous place for a bear alone. He began to clamber back up the
dune. It took a very long time, and once he paused and looked
away along the beach. The waves were rolling in. The wind blew
and Drummond felt very lonely. Where *was* his Sarah? He had to
find her. Until he did, nothing made any sense.

"Sarah!" he called suddenly. "Sar-r-rah!" But his voice blew away and no-one but the circling gulls heard him. Even the dog and its master had passed out of earshot. The world was huge, and frightening, and his Sarah could be anywhere. It was all too much for him. Even Kate was better than this!

"Bears aren't meant to be alone," Drummond told himself as he plodded up the remainder of the dune. He turned sadly back to the white house near the end of the street, no longer a bold adventurer but a small and defeated one.

He managed to creep back into Nicholas' room before anyone was awake to notice the solitary figure returning to his suitcase bed.

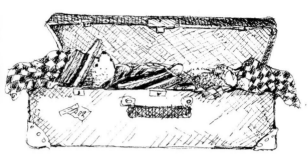

Chapter 10

Kate

I HOPE Drummond doesn't want to come to school again, thought Nicholas. But Drummond didn't.

"What'll you do all day?" asked Nicholas, pulling on his socks.

"I shall probably hibernate. I'm feeling rather tired," said the bear.

Nicholas looked at him curiously, but just then Sarah arrived.

"Well hibernate somewhere safe, then," she said. "We don't want Kate finding you. That would be disastrous! How about the top of Nick's wardrobe?"

Drummond shuddered. "No thank you. One high shelf was more than enough. I shall be quite all right in my bed." And he settled down into the old suitcase.

"Do you want to borrow the book I got from the library?" asked Nicholas. "It's a great story. There's this boy and he gets mixed up with this gang and these..."

"Thank you, but no," cut in the bear. "I have never learned to read. I shall hibernate, as I said." He waved a paw and then became still and, as the children watched, he slowly became stiff and toy-like once more.

"That's *weird*," murmured Nicholas.

"Breakfast!" yelled his mother, as he slid Drummond's suitcase under the bed. He pushed his door shut with his foot and raced away, not noticing the yellow sweater that was trapped against the door jamb.

*   *   *

At half past nine, Kate was bored. Sarah and Nicholas had gone to school and their mother was talking on the telephone. Kate wanted to talk too, but that was not allowed, so she went to play with Polly, who was sleeping in the kitchen with her tail tucked protectively beneath her.

"Don't you want to play, Polly?" asked Kate, trying to rouse the sleepy dog. "Oh well, I'll go and get Miss Prim then."

Kate fetched the doll from her bedroom and was coming back past Nicholas' bedroom door when she noticed his yellow sweater poking out.

"Nick's a naughty boy, leaving his clothes lying about," commented Kate. She put Miss Prim on the carpet and squatted down, tugging at the sweater wedged in the door. It came loose under her fingers, and the door swung open...

For a muzzy moment, Drummond imagined he was on the ship again, because he thought he could hear Sarah singing. They had often passed the time that way when the ship was rolling too much for them to play.

Bye baby bunting, bye baby bunting! sang the voice.

She's forgotten the words, thought Drummond. Sleepily he called out, "Sarah?"

The singing stopped. "I'm not Sarah," the voice said.

Drummond was properly awake now, and worried. There was a little pause as he lay stiff and silent.

"Where are you?" called the voice after a while. "I can't see you."

Drummond shrank further down in his bed.

"Somebody said *Sarah,*" continued the voice. "I'm not Sarah, I'm Kate."

Hearing this, Drummond's eyes opened wide in alarm, and his paws flew up to protect his nose. Kate! The one who pulled the noses off bears — and put bears in the bath!

"I'm looking for you," sang Kate. "I'm looking on the chair."

Drummond quaked.

"Not on the chair. I'll look in the cupboard."

"Ka-ate!" called her mother.

Saved! thought Drummond.

"What, Mum? What, Mum?" The voice faded as the child turned away.

"I just wanted to know where you were."

"In the bedroom! I'm looking for something!" called Kate.

"All right!" replied Mrs Jordan, and Kate turned back towards the room.

It is not all right! thought Drummond, who was very worried by now. But there was nothing he could do but stay totally still.

Footsteps came back into the room. "I'm back," announced Kate. "I'll look in the drawers, now."

There were loud sliding sounds.

61

"Not there," reported Kate. There was a brief silence. "Where are you?" asked the puzzled voice. "Ooh! I'll look under the bed."

Poor Drummond was terrified, as two little black shoes appeared under the edge of the quilt, and were followed by bare knees and hands as Kate knelt down. Her face came into view, hung there for a few seconds, and then smiled. She dragged Drummond's suitcase out from under the bed.

"Ooh, a teddy!" she cried happily. "A teddy with a hat! Have you got ears?" Drummond was lifted from the suitcase, and set quite gently on Kate's lap. And then his hat was lifted off.

"Teddy *has* got ears," said Kate, and she poked her fingers into them to make sure. "And eyes?" she said, peering into Drummond's face. "Now, has Teddy got a nose?" she asked, as she began to prise Drummond's protective paws away from his face.

Drummond had had enough. He swatted wildly at Kate's probing hands. "Don't you *dare* to pull my nose off!" he said angrily.

Kate's face quivered with disbelief. She hurriedly put him down.

"You can...talk?" she gasped.

Drummond glared over his paws, and, as she made no move to attack him again, he slowly lowered them. So this was the Kate he had been warned about! This was the little horror who pulled the noses off bears and put them in the bath!

"I'll give you a kiss," said Kate, after a moment or two. "Would you like a kiss?"

She reached for Drummond again and gave him a kiss between the eyes, which would certainly have knocked his hat off if it hadn't already been on the floor. Even so, he rather liked it.

"Would you like to play?" invited Kate.

Drummond agreed warily that he would. Nobody had really played with him since his Sarah had gone.

"Good." Kate kissed him again.

Drummond was just beginning to enjoy all this attention when Kate asked, "Would you like a bath too?"

"*No!*" he pleaded. "And please don't pull my nose off..."

"All right. I promise," said Kate, handing him back his hat. With a sigh of relief Drummond adjusted it carefully, and gave his new friend a thankful smile. Kate then picked him up and took him to look at the toy chest, leaving the limp Miss Prim forgotten on the floor.

Chapter 11

In the Dark

FTER THAT, Kate and Drummond played together quite
often — but only when Kate's mother was busy. They spent a
lot of time in the back garden, where Kate was allowed to play.
Although she was a clever climber, she had never managed to
climb over the fence. Drummond told her some of the stories which
his Sarah had told him and they had many adventures together in
the following days. The bear could hardly remember when he had
been so happy.

"I think Kate has an imaginary friend," said her mother one
day to the other children when they came home from school. "I
often hear her talking away in the garden, but there's never anyone
there."

Certainly, everyone was surprised at the change in Kate. She no
longer seemed to be forever up to mischief and getting into trouble.
Of course, they had no way of knowing that she had found a
wonderful companion with whom she could spend much of her
time, and was therefore never lonely or bored any more.
Drummond was always careful to be back in his suitcase before the
others came home from school, and Kate certainly didn't tell
anyone about her very special friend. She and Drummond had,
between them, worked out a way to open the bedroom door. They
didn't tell anyone about that either.

Although Sarah and Nick had their suspicions, they couldn't be
sure, until one night when Kate had a bad dream and began to

whimper in her sleep. Sarah opened her eyes. Better get Mum, she thought... but the bedroom door was already opening. Sarah sighed. No need for her to get up now. Her mother had come.

But it wasn't Mrs Jordan who came into the bedroom. At first Sarah couldn't see anyone but, before she had time to get really frightened, a little figure left the shadows of the doorway and walked across the band of moonlight.

It was Drummond.

Under Sarah's astonished gaze the bear grasped a hank of quilt between his front paws and pulled himself up onto Kate's bed. He removed his hat, and put it carefully on the bedside table, and then climbed in beside Kate, who stopped crying, sighed once or twice as she patted the bear, then settled on her side and went back to sleep.

In the morning Drummond was back in his suitcase under Nicholas' bed, so Sarah would have thought she had only dreamed that visit in the dark if it hadn't been for one thing: Drummond wasn't wearing his hat. Sarah found it still on the bedside table where he had placed it before crawling into Kate's bed during the night.

Chapter 12

Fancy Dress

"YOUR AUNT Kath," said Mrs Jordan one Saturday morning, "is incredible." Saturday was the day they got up late and spent as much time as they liked over breakfast. "She's having another party at Hawthorne Hall," Mrs Jordan went on.

"Whatever for?" asked Mr Jordan.

"She says she feels like some more excitement. It's going to be a fancy dress ball for all the local children and their teachers — and anyone else who wants to go along."

"Excitement!" groaned Mr Jordan, who enjoyed a quiet life. "She'll get more than excitement if that lot gets loose. The roof'll fall in. The windows'll get smashed. Tell her not to do it."

"Oh, hush!" replied his wife. "*I* shall go. It's a long time since I went to a party. She's calling it the Mad March Hare Night, and all the proceeds are going to some charity or other. The children will love it."

"Mad's right," said Mr Jordan.

"I'll have to get cracking on costumes for everyone," said Mrs Jordan, determined not to be put off.

*   *   *

When Drummond heard about the party he wanted to go along too.

"After what happened at school?" demanded Nicholas. "You

must be joking!''

Nicholas and Sarah had gone for a walk along the beach — taking Drummond, of course — so they could talk in peace. It was a brisk and breezy day, and there was no-one else about but some interested seagulls, and Polly, darting in front of them after the squawking birds.

''I *must* go,'' insisted Drummond. ''There will be many children there, you said, and dancing. My Sarah loves dancing. Also this will all be happening at the place where you and I first met. So what could be more likely than that my Sarah will be there too?''

Put like that, it did sound logical. ''But it means the sausage bag again,'' warned Nick.

Drummond looked at him complacently. ''Not at all!'' he corrected. ''In fact I shall go along quite openly...as part of a costume! Then when I see my Sarah you shall take me to her, explain how you found me, and that will be that. It is simple.''

''You've got it all worked out, haven't you?'' said Sarah, giving him a little squeeze.

Drummond nodded, feeling very pleased with himself, and returned Sarah's hug.

"And what costume do you plan to be part of?"

"Oh, I shall leave those details to you," said the bear airily. He paused to examine a pink shell. "I shall take this home for my friend Kate," he murmured.

Sarah and Nicholas looked at him in surprise.

"What did you say?" asked Nicholas quietly.

For the first time since the children had known him, Drummond managed to look embarrassed. "Er — I was thinking your charming young sister might enjoy this shell," he said. "Er — perhaps I hadn't mentioned that the dear girl and I have been spending some time together of late?"

"No, perhaps you hadn't," mocked Sarah. Nick squatted down and peered at Drummond's face.

"Well?" said the bear. "What are you looking at?"

"Oh, just checking," said Nicholas. "It's all right. I see you've still got your nose."

"Of course," scoffed Drummond. "You have quite misjudged your sister. She is a very sweet little girl. I like her; she's always nice to me."

Sarah and Nick exchanged surprised looks. Was this the Kate they knew?

*   *   *

And so it was decided that Sarah would dress as a baby for the fancy dress party. She was rather annoyed, as she had intended wearing something more interesting.

"Ghosts don't have teddy bears," Nicholas had argued, "and Mum has already made my ghost suit."

Mrs Jordan was rather surprised about Sarah's choice. "But it won't be too difficult to make a baby's costume," she said. "You can wear one of my nighties and some bedsocks for bootees, and I'll see if I can find a rattle and knit you a bonnet."

So that's what they did. Kate was to stay home with her father, as she was still a bit too young for a night out.

When they arrived at Hawthorne Hall on the evening of the party, the house was almost bulging with children.

''Hello Nick. Hello Sarah,'' said Mrs Harrington-Edwards, striding towards them. She was in costume too, and loving it all. ''Now off you hop into the big room. You'll find some of your friends in there.''

And they certainly did. That is, they saw three Spanish ladies, five gypsy girls, a Queen of Hearts and two jesters. There were three other ghosts as well, and soon Nicholas had darted off to compare groans with his rivals. Unfortunately, the noisiest ghost

turned out to be Ronald McKeever, who managed to stamp on the bottom of Nick's costume with a very un-ghostly boot.

"Look, there's another teddy bear!" said Sarah, pointing to an enormous one. "I think it's Uncle David pretending he isn't here."

Drummond couldn't answer in such a public place, so Sarah began to scan the room for anyone who could possibly be Drummond's Sarah. It was quite difficult. A great many of the girls had hoods or hats or wigs, and those who did have long brown hair seemed to be wearing masks or make-up. One Indian princess looked quite promising, but when Sarah had pushed her way through the squealing, sliding mass of children, she found that the girl had brown eyes to match her hair, not the beautiful blue eyes Drummond claimed his Sarah possessed. A long-haired pirate turned out to be a boy in his sister's wig, and two ballerinas were much too fat. So now Sarah was perched on a seat, dangling her legs and holding Drummond where he could see the crowd. Uncle David had put on a record, and people were beginning to dance. Suddenly a witch, arm in arm with a broomstick, arrived in front of her. The witch was Miss Honey, and the broomstick, whose bristle head-dress almost brushed the chandeliers, was Mr Pearce.

Sarah smiled "Hello" uneasily. It felt funny to see a teacher away from the school, and in fancy costume at that. Miss Honey must have guessed what she was thinking. "They do let us out sometimes, Sarah!" she laughed.

Sarah giggled nervously.

"I see you've brought along your brother's friend," said Mr Pearce. It took Sarah some seconds to realise that he was talking about Drummond.

"May I?" Mr Pearce stretched out his hand. "Thank you. Hmm, he's really a very fine example of craftsmanship. They really knew how to make toys in those days."

"What days?" asked Sarah blankly.

"I should say this fellow was made about eighty or ninety years ago. Look at the details of the costume," invited Mr Pearce,

handing Drummond over to Miss Honey. Sarah began to feel cross was well as nervous. It was as if they had forgotten all about her!

"What I find most impressive is this watch," Miss Honey was telling Mr Pearce. "It's a real one in miniature. Probably silver. A collector's item."

"Could I have him back now?" asked Sarah, holding out her hand in turn. Reluctantly, Miss Honey handed Drummond back.

"Shall we dance, then?" asked Mr Pearce, and the witch and the broomstick whirled away, leaving Sarah thoughtful and indignant.

"You never told me you were so old!" she whispered to Drummond.

"Old? Me? Nonsense!" said the bear. "The man's mistaken. I don't think he knows what he's talking about."

"But he's a teacher!" said Sarah.

"That doesn't mean he knows everything about bears," whispered Drummond, trying to hold back a smile.

"He knows a lot about toys," said Sarah.

"And I know a lot about *me*," said Drummond. "You don't think I'm old, do you?"

"Of course not, Drummond dear," Sarah replied quickly. But she wasn't sure.

They sat in silence for a while, watching a roomful of people stamping and shouting through a noisy dance — wizards, princes, Red Riding Hoods, snowmen, Supermen, robots, monsters and ghosts. Sarah couldn't even be certain which of the ghost costumes contained her brother, so what chance did she have of spotting one young girl she had never met? Could that Robin Hood be Drummond's Sarah? Or that nurse? Sarah wished she could dance with the others, and was just wondering whether Drummond would object when she felt her sleeve being violently tugged.

"What?" she asked in a low voice.

Drummond strained forward in her arms. "Over there!" he hissed. "Look. By the table... I think it's *her!* My Sarah!"

Chapter 13

The Girl in the White Pinafore

SARAH PEERED anxiously through the dancers to the table where the covered plates of refreshments waited. "Do you mean the girl in that old-fashioned white dress?" she asked.

Drummond nodded, trembling with eagerness. "Yes, in the pinafore," he agreed. "Sensible girl! She hasn't bothered to wear a special costume, to be sure I would recognise her!"

Sarah glanced at Drummond curiously. The girl certainly *was* wearing a costume. She looked like the picture of Mary Lennox in her book of the *The Secret Garden*.

"Take me to her now!" pleaded Drummond.

Sarah rose to her feet. Of course it would be lovely for Drummond to go home to his real Sarah, but what about the Jordans? "We'll miss you terribly, Drummond," she whispered to him sadly, but the bear scarcely listened.

"Oh well," said Sarah, and began to pick her way over towards the table. She had to watch where she put her feet, for some of the ghosts were having sliding games on the slippery dance-floor.

"Please hurry!" urged Drummond, and Sarah hurried, although the crowded room made it very difficult. But somehow, when they reached the table, the girl had disappeared.

Drummond let out a wail of dismay, and several people turned to stare curiously at Sarah. She tried to look as if she had made the noise herself, and gazed around, hoping to see where the girl had gone.

"Have you seen a girl in a white pinafore?" she asked the nearest adult.

"No, I'm afraid not, my dear," said the woman.

"She was here just a minute ago," pleaded Sarah. The woman shook her head.

"Anything wrong, Sarah?" asked Mrs Harrington-Edwards, who was just passing by.

Sarah tried to sound natural. "I was looking for a girl, Aunt Kath."

"Plenty to pick from," commented Mrs Harrington-Edwards. "More girls than boys."

"Yes, but this one was standing here a minute ago," continued Sarah. "She had a white dress on. Drumm...er, someone said it

was a pinafore she was wearing. And she had long brown hair in curls. I think her name was Sarah.''

Her great-aunt smiled. ''Well, I'll keep my eyes peeled,'' she promised. ''Having a good time?''

Sarah nodded.

''Still got your teddy, I see,'' Mrs Harrington-Edwards noted, nodding at Drummond.

''Yes, he's part of my costume,'' said Sarah. ''Aunt Kath...two of the teachers at our school seem to think he's quite special. Did you know he had a real watch in his pocket?''

''No! Really?'' Sarah's great-aunt looked surprised and interested, but at that moment her husband, still in his bear costume, came lumbering over to her side to say he was running out of dancing-type records, and to ask when supper would begin. ''I'm as hungry as a *bear!*'' he growled loudly, patting his large padded stomach.

People nearby heard him and laughed and Mrs Harrington-Edwards turned away. ''Supper will be at half past eight, if you can *bear* to wait that long!'' she said loudly, and everyone laughed again.

Sarah backed away from the table and climbed on a chair to have a good look over the crowded room. Was that a flash of white over in the corner? It was, but when she reached it, it turned out to be one of the ghosts, quietly eating a large piece of cream cake. ''Oh, Nick!'' said Sarah accusingly.

Nicholas looked up sulkily. ''I got hungry, and Ronald McKeever kept treading on my ghost suit,'' he explained. ''What have you been doing, anyway?''

''Trying to find Drummond's Sarah.''

Nick shot upright and almost choked, spraying crumbs out at all angles. ''What?'' he gasped, between coughs. ''Without me?''

''You were busy sliding on the floor,'' his sister pointed out.

''Er-hm!'' said Drummond crossly. ''Can't you two quarrel some other time?''

74

"Well, where is this Sarah? What's she like? Does she want Drummond back?" gabbled Nicholas, wiping his creamy fingers on his costume.

"Drummond thought he saw her by the table, but when we got there she'd gone," explained Sarah.

Just then Drummond tugged at her sleeve again. *"There!"* he cried, and Sarah looked round to see the girl in the white pinafore slipping out of the room, followed by a woman in a long, trailing costume.

"There she goes! Hurry, oh hurry!" cried Drummond.

Sarah and Nicholas pushed through the crowd. The door through which their quarry had vanished led into the entrance hall. It was empty, and the front door was closed. "Hurry!" urged Drummond again, as they rushed to the door.

The wide verandah was empty, and so too, except for the rows of parked cars and the faint outlines of their great-aunt's horses beyond the fence, were the grounds.

"Gone!" moaned Drummond.

But Nicholas disagreed. He pushed back his pillowcase hood with the blackened eye-holes and looked about intently, like detectives do on television. "None of those cars has been started up," he pointed out. "And there just hasn't been enough time for her to have made her getaway."

"Maybe she came on a bicycle," suggested Sarah vaguely. "Oh-no, I suppose she couldn't have. Her mum's dress was too long for her to be riding a bicycle."

"That couldn't have been her mother," said Drummond. "My Sarah doesn't have a mother!"

"Well, her aunt then, or whoever she was. They went out together."

"They're not here, anyway," said Nicholas, and they went back into the hallway, just in time to see the girl and the older woman coming out of the downstairs bathroom and heading back into the big room.

"Hey!" yelled Nicholas, but the music from the open door drowned his voice.

"This is like hide-and-seek," said Sarah breathlessly, as the white pinafore disappeared once again into the crowd.

The music stopped abruptly, and Mrs Harrington-Edwards began directing everyone over to the laden supper tables. "There!" said Nick, burrowing through a solid wall of people.

"Oh, there you are," said their mother cheerfully, grabbing them. "I haven't seen you all evening. Come and have something to eat."

"But we've got to find Sarah!" explained Nicholas excitedly, pulling away from his mother's grasp.

"There's Sarah right beside you!" said Mrs Jordan impatiently. "Now come on!"

"Not *her*. We're looking for *another* Sarah! We have to talk to her."

"Well you can do that later," said his mother firmly. She made the children stay beside her until most people began to move away from the now almost empty food tables.

"Help!" said Nicholas. "We'll never catch up with her now!"

"Oh yes we will!" vowed Sarah. "We'll wait near the door. Then she can't go out without us seeing her."

This seemed like a good idea, so they slipped away, while their mother was getting herself a second cup of tea, and took up their positions, one on either side of the door. But somehow it was difficult to keep their attention on everyone, as the people were beginning to leave, sometimes in groups of five or six. Miss Honey and Mr Pearce stopped to say goodbye to them, and it was while Mr Pearce was saying again how lucky they were to have such a fine teddy bear that the girl in the white pinafore and the woman in the trailing dress went out of the door.

"Hey!" yelled Nicholas, and the girl turned around. Miss Honey and Mr Pearce moved on to say goodnight to Mrs Harrington-Edwards and the children noticed, with relief, that the girl said something to the woman beside her and came back towards them.

"Mrs Harrington-Edwards said someone was looking for me," she said. "Was that you?"

Nicholas nodded, and pulled off his ghost hood so he could see her better. Now that the moment had come, the children were not quite sure what to do. Sarah decided to let Drummond handle it in his own way, and held him out with a tentative smile.

"What do you want?" asked the girl, ignoring Drummond.

"We thought...er...well... someone said you'd lost a bear."

Sarah waggled Drummond to get the girl's attention. "This bear. Is he yours?"

The girl looked puzzled, frowned and shook her head. "No," she replied, giving Sarah a strange look. "I haven't lost a bear."

"But..." Sarah looked down at Drummond, who stared back with the saddest look she had ever seen in his small brown eyes.

"Aren't you Sarah?" asked Nicholas.

The girl shook her head again. "My name's Jennie," she said, "And I told you, I haven't lost any bears."

"Oh, sorry," said Nicholas.

"We thought you were somebody else," explained Sarah. The girl hovered for a moment or two, then gave them a friendly little nod and went away.

Nicholas turned accusingly to Sarah. "You said that was Sarah!" he said.

"No, Drummond said it was," corrected Sarah.

They looked expectantly at Drummond, who was drooping in

Sarah's grasp. They hardly expected him to answer in a public place, but the bear surprised them. "Not my Sarah! Not my Sarah! Oh dear, where is my Sarah?"

"Did you catch up with your friend?" demanded a brisk voice, and Mrs Harrington-Edwards was beside them.

"I told her you wanted to see her."

And that was when it happened. One of those sudden silences fell, and into it, clearly and unmistakeably, dropped the voice of the bear.

"How could I have made such a mistake?" moaned Drummond.

Before the startled gaze of Mrs Harrington-Edwards, and the curious eyes of four people who were leaving the party at that moment, the bear in Sarah's hands lifted both front paws and put them sadly over its eyes.

"Isn't it amazing what they can make toys do nowadays?" said Mrs Harrington-Edwards hurriedly, after she had recovered from her surprise. But she didn't sound too sure. "Your mother is ready to go now, children, but she has kindly offered to come and help me clear up tomorrow morning. Want to come back too?"

Nicholas threw an agonised glance at Sarah, who shrugged her shoulders back at him. "Thank you Aunt Kath," she said woodenly. "We'd like that."

79

Chapter 14

Mrs Harrington-Edwards

THERE WAS no chance to talk with Drummond that night, as their mother sent them straight to bed when they returned home. Sarah handed Drummond over to Nicholas, who put him carefully to bed in his suitcase. The bear had neither moved nor spoken since they left the fancy dress party, and nor did he the next morning when the children met hurriedly in Nicholas' room before breakfast.

"It's all your fault," accused Nicholas bitterly. "You were the one that said you'd found Sarah."

"I did not!" said Sarah indignantly. "Drummond thought it was her."

"Well it wasn't, was it?" said Nicholas sulkily. "And it was you that let on to Aunt Kath."

"I did not!"

"You did! You must have! That girl knew we were looking for her!"

"I had to do something. You weren't any help," retorted Sarah. "All you did was play stupid games with those stupid boys!"

Sarah and Nicholas glared at each other. It was the sort of argument that might have gone on for ages. They didn't feel like spending the morning together, but they had to. Their mother would see to that. And besides, there was Drummond. What were they going to do about him?

In the end, they took him along in the car to their great-aunt's

house when they went with their mother to help clean up after the party. "Then if Aunt Kath says something, we've got some proof," observed Nicholas. Sarah, who hadn't forgiven him for blaming her, merely grunted and, when they reached Hawthorne Hall, it was Kate who quietly removed Drummond and carried him off to play in the garden. She slipped round behind one of Mrs Harrington-Edwards' garden sheds and set Drummond down on the grass.

"Now teddy, tell me about the party, please," she asked her friend, but the bear remained as stiff as any other toy. Kate picked him up and cuddled him, but it was no use. He gave no sign of life whatsoever. Kate was puzzled and disappointed.

*   *   *

Hawthorne Hall looked very different this morning, with the slightly forlorn air of tattered streamers and a lonely Superman cape in the hall. Mrs Jordan vacuumed the floors, while Nicholas and Sarah picked up all the odd bits of paper and shredded napkins and bruised flowers that lay about under the table and behind the doors. Because they were not speaking to one another, it was some time before they realised that neither of them had Drummond.

"That teddy bear?" said their mother mildly when they asked if she'd seen Drummond. "I think I saw Kate with it earlier."

"Well, you shouldn't have let her take him. He's ours!" complained Nicholas.

"I hardly think she'll damage it," said Mrs Jordan. "And if you didn't want your little sister to play with it you shouldn't have left it where she could get it."

Since Nicholas knew this already, it made him even more cross to be reminded. He went and told Sarah all about it, but Sarah just shrugged. She was still annoyed with her brother, and also worried about what questions Aunt Kath might ask about the extraordinary bear whom she had definitely heard speaking the night before. Sarah was wishing that her great-aunt would hurry up and say something and get it over with. The thought even touched her mind that if Kate managed to lose Drummond out in the grounds of Hawthorne Hall they might all be better off. No more embarrassing happenings. And, as for Drummond, he would hardly feel any worse than he obviously did now after such a disappointment with the girl in the white pinafore.

It didn't take long to make the place all tidy again, and by twelve o'clock Mrs Jordan was ready to leave. "Just go and round up Kate, will you please Sarah?" she said. "And then we'll be off."

"Oh, you can all stay and have lunch with me if you like," said Mrs Harrington-Edwards.

"Oh, thanks all the same, but I've got too much to do at

home," replied Mrs Jordan. "Nick and Sarah can stay though, if they want to," she added.

So Nicholas and Sarah — and Drummond too, when they had prised him loose from Kate — stayed.

"Well," said Mrs Harrington-Edwards when they were at last alone. "I want a word with you two. But we'll eat first, eh?"

They had their lunch out on the grass, watched by the horses from the other side of the garden fence.

"Now then, you two," she said at last, while pouring tea, "I'm pretty sure you know what I want to talk about, don't you?"

"It's about Drummond, isn't it?" said Sarah nervously.

"Who — or what — is Drummond?" asked Mrs Harrington-Edwards.

"This teddy bear you gave us," said Nick, pointing to the lifeless Drummond lying beside them on the grass.

Their great-aunt sipped her tea and peered at them thoughtfully. "Not to beat about the bush," she said, "I know what I saw — and heard — last night. What I still haven't got clear is who — or what — was responsible for it."

The children looked back at her blankly.

"Oh, come on!" said Mrs Harrington-Edwards. "Either one of you is a very talented ventriloquist and puppeteer, or there is something very funny about that bear. Or else I'm hearing and seeing things. Which is it?"

Sarah and Nicholas looked at one another in dismay. "We're really not supposed to tell anyone," said Sarah.

"Hmmm, I take it it *is* the bear, then. What is it — mechanical? The reason I'm asking is partly because someone else was asking me about it last night."

"A girl?" asked Sarah eagerly.

Mrs Harrington-Edwards shook her head. "No, two teachers from your school. It seems they think your bear — Drummond? — might be quite valuable, and they wanted to know where I got it and how long I'd had it and so forth. Of course I couldn't help

83

them much. And then they asked if I had considered donating it to a toy museum.''

Nicholas almost choked with indignation, but his great-aunt held up her hand. ''Naturally, I told them the bear wasn't mine to donate,'' she said. ''But all the same, I'd like to know what's going on.''

''It's a secret,'' said Nicholas, ''Nobody knows about Drummond except us two.''

''And Kate,'' added Sarah.

''Kate too?''

''Yes, she found him once when she was poking about in my bedroom,'' explained Nicholas.

''But why is it such a secret? Surely you didn't think I'd ask for it back if I knew it was such a special bear?''

The children shook their heads. ''Some people might, but we knew you'd never do that,'' said Sarah quietly.

''Well, why then? Or did you just like having a secret? Because if that's all it is, I shall say no more about it.''

They thought about this. It was tempting, but Sarah felt as if she owed Aunt Kath at least a part explanation. ''We thought . . . we sort of expected...'' she began, and couldn't think how to continue.

Nicholas chipped in, ''We thought if other children found out, they'd want him too, and if grown-ups did they'd take him away and perhaps pull him to bits!''

''Thank you Nicholas. But what, precisely, is there to find out? And I assure you *I* won't pull him to bits, whatever it is.''

''He *talks*,'' announced Nicholas. ''And *walks*!''

''Clockwork?'' asked Mrs Harrington-Edwards.

Sarah shook her head. ''That's what we thought, at first, but he hasn't got a key. He's...sort of...''

''*Alive!*'' whispered Nicholas.

Chapter 15

The Silent Bear

IT WAS the first time they had said it to anyone but each other, and it was a very odd feeling indeed. In fact, it made Sarah giggle nervously as she saw the astonished look on her great-aunt's face.

"But I don't expect you to believe us," she added.

"Easily checked," said Mrs Harrington-Edwards, looking at them expectantly. "Introduce us, please," she suggested.

"This is our Aunt Kath, Drummond. She's the lady who gave you to us," said Nicholas immediately.

Both children waited to see what Drummond would do. He remained lifeless.

"Hey, Drummond!" said Nicholas, in a louder voice. But, as before, there was no response.

They tried for some time, urging, pleading and almost ordering, but Drummond still lay on his back in the grass, with his paws sticking up in the air. He looked just like any old teddy bear.

Sarah felt her face getting hot, as if she had been caught telling lies. Nicholas was getting angry. 'Why won't he talk?" he demanded.

"I don't know what's wrong," said Sarah to Mrs Harrington-Edwards. "He *does* talk usually. I mean, we aren't just making it up."

"I know you're not. I heard him last night. I wonder, though. Are you certain it wasn't a radio or a tape recording you were

listening to?''

Sarah and Nicholas shook their heads. They were quite sure.

"But I've just thought of one thing," added Sarah. "Don't you remember, Nick, he said once he didn't talk in front of grown-ups?"

"That's right! That first night we had him!" agreed Nicholas.

"Seems like I'll have to do without my proof," said Mrs Harrington-Edwards. "But you can still tell me all about it, can't you, now that I know this much?"

The children decided they could. Aunt Kath was all right. Aunt Kath would never tell.

"All I can suggest is that we put a notice in the paper," said Mrs Harrington Edwards when she had heard the whole story. "You know the sort of thing. IF DRUMMOND'S FRIEND SARAH WRITES TO THIS ADDRESS SHE MAY HEAR SOMETHING TO HER ADVANTAGE."

This seemed such a brilliantly simple idea that the children wondered why they hadn't thought of it for themselves. "But we'd never have been able to pay for it, would we?" pointed out Sarah.

"I'll take care of it, then," said their great-aunt briskly. "And now I'll run you home, and you can pass on the glad tidings to Drummond when all grown-ups are safely out of the way."

When they got home they avoided their mother and took Drummond straight to Sarah's bedroom to tell him the latest news. But, though they called his name, clapped their hands and even shook him, the bear neither moved nor spoke.

"And he's not just pretending, like he did at school, either," said Nicholas uneasily. "He's really out of it."

"Drummond — Drummond! We're trying to find your Sarah! Drummond!" cried Sarah. She might just as well have been talking to Miss Prim. The bear made no reply.

"I'll go and get Kate," decided Nicholas. "He seems to like her best."

"Yes, do," agreed Sarah, and Nicholas went away to find

his small sister.

He returned with Kate, who climbed into the bed beside Drummond. She looked warily from her brother and sister to the bear and back again. "I didn't hurt teddy, did I?" she asked.

"No, of course you didn't!" said Sarah. She knelt down in front of Kate. "Kate, do you know who Drummond is?"

Kate nodded. "Teddy," she said.

"He's a nice teddy, isn't he?" said Sarah.

Kate nodded again. "Teddy...teddy talks," she blurted. "Teddy walks too. Like this." She scrambled off the bed and moved a few paces across the room with her knees stiff and her arms held slightly away from her body.

"Did teddy talk to you at Aunt Kath's today?" asked Sarah. But Kate wouldn't answer and, when Sarah persisted, she began suddenly to cry.

"What's the matter with her?" asked Nicholas, as Kate ran out of the room.

"I don't know," said Sarah. "Unless she thinks it's her fault he won't talk."

"Maybe it is," said Nicholas.

"No, I think he won't talk because he's disappointed about last night. He probably needs a good rest. Let's put him in his suitcase."

So they did.

*   *   *

At first they got up every morning expecting Drummond to have woken up with some cross words about the fancy dress party, but day followed day and still the bear remained stiff and silent.

"Maybe he'll never wake up," said Sarah sadly. "Not until we find his friend, anyway."

She sighed then, because they were no nearer to finding the other Sarah at all. Mrs Harrington-Edwards had put the advertisement in the newspaper as she had promised, but there had been no reply to it and, though she had also asked around her friends, nothing new had come up. "The only thing is," she told Sarah one afternoon, "I *did* manage to locate the woman who brought him along to the stall in the first place."

Sarah pricked up her ears at that. Drummond had always seemed to think that Hawthorne Hall was the house where he had been left by his Sarah. This, apparently, was not the case.

"And?" she asked eagerly.

"Dead end, I'm afraid," said Mrs Harrington-Edwards. "Someone had heard I was collecting and had given him to her for me."

"But *someone* must remember!" exclaimed Sarah. "It was only a few weeks ago, after all!"

"You'd think so, wouldn't you?" said her great-aunt. "I'll let you know if I find out anything. Perhaps the real Sarah will turn up at this year's Teddy Bears' Picnic, up at Mrs Askland's Tea Gardens."

But Sarah wasn't listening. She had the sad feeling that, if nothing happened soon, Drummond would stay forever the way he was now...just another lifeless, yellow teddy bear.

NOTICE TO PARENTS

There will be a special excursion to the Teddy Bears' Picnic at the Tea Gardens on the Wednesday before Easter, under the supervision of Miss Honey and Mr Pearce.

Buses will leave the school at 1.00 p.m., returning by 3.30 p.m.

A limited number of seats will be available for any parents and younger children who might wish to attend.

Chapter 16

Teddy Bears' Picnic

DRUMMOND ALMOST didn't go to the Teddy Bears' Picnic. Even before he had nearly given the whole secret away at the Fancy Dress Party, Sarah and Nicholas had decided that they could really look for Drummond's Sarah as well without Drummond as with him. "Better," said Nicholas, "if we don't have to bother about keeping him quiet."

So they left him in his suitcase under Nicholas' bed and went off to school.

But the schoolchildren weren't the only ones going on the excursion to the Teddy Bears' Picnic. Teddy bear fanciers were coming from near and far, and parents had been invited to bring their younger children as well.

Kate was very excited. She knew a big bus would be taking her to a place where there would be lots of teddy bears, and she wondered if any of *these* bears would want to talk to her, like Drummond did. She fussed and fretted all morning, and straight after lunch she was all ready, waiting by the door, with Drummond tucked firmly under her arm.

Mrs Jordan didn't notice until they boarded the bus, and by then it was too late.

"Teddy's coming too," said Kate.

"I can see that," said her mother. "But you'll have to hold on to him and make sure he doesn't get lost."

Kate beamed and assured her mother that she would take great

care of the bear.

The Forest Grove Tea Gardens were not very far from Hawthorne but, since they were on top of a steep hill, it took some time for the buses to grind and groan their way up the winding road.

"What a crowd!" said Mrs Jordan as she lifted Kate down the steps. She was right. Cars were everywhere, and there seemed to be hundreds of schoolchildren, a few parents and younger brothers and sisters, and several older people as well.

The Tearoom itself was a new white building which fairly blazed with glass against the dark background of the trees. The gardens were full of winding mossy paths, rockeries, little ponds, banks of flowers and sudden small patches of lawn where white iron tables stood. Most of the people were heading for a wide grassy area in front of the Tearoom, where there was a vast tarpaulin on which sat rows and rows of teddy bears.

"Come and see the teddies, Kate," invited Mrs Jordan, holding out her hand. Kate nodded, her bright eyes taking in everything.

Miss Honey, Nicholas' teacher, was already standing by the ranks of bears, supervising the children who wished to put their own toys on display or to admire the others. Each bear on the tarpaulin wore a numbered badge of cardboard. "So that they don't get mixed up," explained Miss Honey.

A few of the toys were sitting up on a table, with sheets of cardboard propped against them, telling where and when they had been made, who they had belonged to, and giving their names.

"Goodness," said Mrs Jordan, "look at all the different sorts and colours, Kate. Which one do you like best?"

"I like Drummond," said Kate, hugging him closely.

And that was when Nicholas, who had been messing about near the fishpond, noticed Kate — and what Kate had brought with her. He glared indignantly at his mother. It always made him feel funny when Mrs Jordan appeared at any school function. He sometimes had nightmares in which Miss Honey and his mother

were each trying to make him do something quite different at the same time. And it was even worse to see Kate there. Kate was sure to do something horrible.

"What's up?" asked Sarah, stopping to see what Nick was looking at.

"There," he said, pointing to his little sister.

"Mum and Kate. So what?" Sarah didn't mind mixing school and home.

"Yes, but look what she's got!"

"Oh. Drummond."

"Yes. Drummond!" Nicholas began to hop with impatience. "We'll have to get him away from her!"

Sarah didn't agree. "He hasn't done anything for days and days, so he isn't likely to come out of his hibernation now, all of a sudden."

"But, what if he does?"

"I suppose we'll just have to keep an eye on him then," said Sarah. As they watched, their mother and Kate went up to a white haired woman and asked her something. The woman smiled, and pointed toward the back of the Tearoom, and Mrs Jordan and Kate went off in the direction the woman had indicated.

The children were following, when Nicholas suddenly put out a

hand to stop Sarah. "Look!" he whispered. "That woman is staring suspiciously at Drummond. I think she's planning to steal him!"

"Don't be silly," scoffed Sarah, "That's Mrs Askland. She owns this place. Why would she want to steal anyone's teddy?"

"Well, someone might. I bet Miss Honey would like to have him. So would Mr Pearce."

Now that Sarah came to think of it, grown-ups did seem to be particularly interested in Drummond, even though they didn't know how special he really was. "I suppose this would be the place to steal a bear if you were planning to," she agreed. "But Mr Pearce wouldn't."

"He might pay someone else to do it for him," said Nicholas. "Like that woman. Look, she's still staring . . . no she isn't. I

know! She knows we're watching her and she's playing safe!"

"N-i-c-k! You watch too much television," drawled Sarah.

He had to agree that his idea really wasn't a very likely one. All the same, he decided to keep an eye on Kate and Drummond. It wasn't very easy, because his teacher seemed to be keeping an eye on *him.*

"And just where are you off to, Nicholas Jordan?" Miss Honey asked, as Nicholas trailed Kate and his mother down one of the mossy paths. "You know you're supposed to stay with the rest of the group."

Nicholas looked around warily. Then he had an idea. He'd tell the truth . . . well, part of the truth. "I'm looking for my sister, Miss Honey," he said innocently.

"Are you *supposed* to be looking after her?" asked Miss Honey. She disapproved of mixing home and school almost as much as Nicholas did.

"Oh no," replied Nicholas. "But she's got our bear, and I want to make sure he's safe."

Miss Honey looked interested. "I wondered if you'd brought him. You know, he really ought to be up on the table with all the other special ones, just for today. Would you like that?"

"Not really," said Nicholas, trying not to look alarmed at the thought. "And Kate would yell. I didn't bring the bear — *she* did."

"Oh, I see. Well you get back to your group now Nicholas, please. I think we can rely on your mother to keep an eye on your bear for you."

You don't know Mum, thought Nicholas to himself, but he didn't say so. Nevertheless, he kept a close watch on the top of the path taken by his mother and Kate and was intrigued to see the white haired woman slipping down it. Aha! thought Nicholas. I knew it! He glanced round for Miss Honey, but she was busy answering questions from Rebecca Anderson. So he stuck his hands in his pockets, and began to stroll along as if he wasn't going

anywhere in particular — straight down the path.

"*Nicholas!*" called Miss Honey, and this time she pulled him back by the arm.

Nicholas sulked, and wondered whether Miss Honey could possibly have eyes in the back of her head.

Everyone had afternoon tea after that, and Mrs Askland made a speech of welcome. She explained why she was holding the Teddy Bears' Picnic at her Tea Gardens.

"People often ask me why I like teddy bears so much," she began. "And sometimes I tell them one thing and sometimes I tell them another, but really it's because a favourite teddy bear is like an old friend. You can tell him anything! He's good at keeping secrets, too!"

Everyone laughed at that, and Mrs Askland laughed too.

"I know just how wonderful a teddy bear can be. I'm going to tell you a story now, that happened a long, long time ago — when I wasn't any older than you children.

"My mother died when I was very small, and I was looked after by my aunt, my father's sister. We lived in another country at that time, and my father decided to come here to live. You see, his brother was already here, and he sent for Father to help him with his business. Aunt was going to come with us but, not long before we left, she decided to get married, so in the end only my father and I came. It took a long time to get here on the ship — ships weren't as fast then as they are now, and I really would have been very lonely and unhappy if it hadn't been for a present my aunt gave me for my birthday just before we left."

"What was it?" yelled someone from the back.

Mrs Askland smiled again. "Can anyone guess?"

Nicholas' mouth was feeling very dry and peculiar. He tried to make himself say something, but another voice got in first. Nicholas wasn't in the least surprised to realise that the voice belonged to his sister Sarah.

"Was the present a . . . a teddy bear?" she asked.

Chapter 17

The Other Sarah

"THAT'S RIGHT!" said Mrs Askland. "It was a teddy bear. And thanks to that gift from Aunt Helen the voyage wasn't so bad. It was not an ordinary bear, you know, because Aunt Helen had had him made specially. They did sometimes make toys by hand in those days. This one was wonderful, and I used to sit and play with him and talk with him by the hour on board that ship. It was almost as good as having a brother or a sister. My father had told me a good deal about this country, and so I told it all to my friend.

"Even when I was grown up and married I always liked teddy bears, and now that I'm old I can collect them and nobody's ever rude enough to tell me I'm being silly! So thank you to all you people who brought your bears along today. And as for the people who didn't — well, why don't you promise yourselves that you'll bring them along to *next* year's Teddy Bears' Picnic?"

There was quite a burst of applause when Mrs Askland had finished, and Nicholas noticed that even some of the older people, who had been sitting on the white iron chairs, had come over to hear what she had to say. But less than half of his mind was thinking like that. The other half was running in frantic circles, like water in a whirlpool. It *can't* be, said his mind. Can it? Of course it can't! After all, lots of people used to come here on ships, and most of them probably brought toys with them. And, anyway, Mrs Askland came so long ago. It *can't* be!

And then Nicholas heard his sister ask Mrs Askland if she still had that bear.

"No, unfortunately I haven't," said Mrs Askland sadly. "However, I can show you what he looked like! Would you like that?"

Several people nodded their heads, or called out "Yes!", so Mrs Askland turned and went into the Tearoom. She was back in only a few moments, carrying a silver frame.

The rest of the crowd craned to see, but Nicholas and Sarah knew just what was in that frame. It was a large, old-fashioned photograph, with rather milky edges, and it showed a small girl with smiling eyes and long, glossy, curling hair.

The child was looking straight at the camera, and, in her lap, she held a teddy bear who wore a smart waistcoat, a blazer and a straw hat. There was a watch-chain looped across the front of the waistcoat.

Neither Nicholas nor Sarah doubted for a second that the bear in the picture was Drummond. The only question was — what were they going to do about it?

"We'll have to give him back, of course," said Sarah, when they had all finished eating and the two had got together to discuss this unexpected turn of events.

Nicholas was not sure that he agreed. "She did go and leave Drummond behind in that room," he pointed out. "That's if it *was* Drummond."

"Of course it was!" snapped Sarah.

"But the time's all wrong!" said Nicholas. "Drummond only got left a few weeks ago, not years and years back."

"You know how he hibernates though," said Sarah. "He must have just gone to sleep and not woken up until that day at Aunt Kath's Village Fair when he heard you calling out my name. So we'd better get him from Kate and show him to Mrs Askland."

"Even so, she went away and left him," insisted Nicholas. "I think she's horrible. She must be, to have done a thing like that."

"You'd think so, but we might be wrong," said Sarah. "We were wrong about Kate, weren't we?"

"How?"

"We thought she'd pull Drummond's nose off, but she didn't. Anyhow, we've got to talk to Mrs Askland," said Sarah.

Reluctantly, Nicholas agreed. "I think she suspects already. I saw her following Kate earlier, trying to get a good look at Drummond ... when you said I'd been watching too much television, because I thought she might have been trying to steal him."

"Well, let's find Kate first," said Sarah.

So they looked around for their little sister. But they found Mrs Askland first.

"Excuse me ..." began Sarah.

The white haired woman turned and smiled. "Yes?"

"Excuse me ... we wondered ... we wanted to know ..."

Once more Nicholas put a bald question. Scowling but determined, he tapped Mrs Askland on the elbow and asked her if her first name was, by any chance, Sarah.

Mrs Askland blinked. Plenty of people had asked her questions that day, but not this one. "Yes dear, it is," she said. "How did you know?"

"We thought it must be," said Nicholas, sadly.

Miss Honey arrived just then, and loomed over Nicholas and Sarah. "I hope these two aren't bothering you," she said, and Mrs Askland shook her head.

"Come along," said Miss Honey, taking Nicholas by the arm. "We're all going down the garden to play some games now."

"But we've got to talk to Mrs Askland! It's important!"

"Come *along*, Nicholas," Miss Honey insisted.

Sarah could see their chance to talk with the other Sarah sliding away. Then she remembered how interested Miss Honey had been in Drummond.

"We were just going to show our teddy bear to Mrs Askland," she pleaded. "We thought she might be interested."

Mrs Askland smiled politely. "I'm sure he's a lovely one dear, but you'd better run along with the others now."

"I thought your little sister had him?" said Miss Honey.

"We were just going to get him," explained Nicholas.

"We thought Mrs Askland might really like to see Drummond," said Sarah, "because he looks a bit like the one she showed us in the picture."

"Yes, he does, really," agreed Miss Honey. "Well, don't be too long."

When she had gone, the children turned back to Mrs Askland. She was staring at them strangely.

"Did I hear you say *Drummond*? I think we'd better go into the office," she said softly.

"Yes, I'll go and get him from Kate," said Sarah.

Mrs Askland shook her head. "Not yet, please." She turned

silently away and led them through the Tearoom into a cosy office at the back of the building. She sat down, and told the children to do the same.

For a moment they all stared at one another.

"So it *was* Drummond that the little girl had after all?" said Mrs Askland, partly to herself.

"I knew it. You *were* following Kate!" exclaimed Nicholas.

The old woman nodded. "My eyes aren't what they were," she explained. "But that bear looked so familiar. I never really thought it was him, just that it might be another one made at the same time. How long have you had him? Where did you get him from?"

Sarah and Nicholas took it in turns to explain how Drummond had come to them, and they found themselves going on to tell about the unfortunate first day at school, the attempts to hide the bear from Kate, and about the fancy dress party.

"Well, he *has* led you a run-around!" said Mrs Askland. "You poor things."

"He was only looking for *you*," replied Sarah. "Because he thinks ... he thought ..." To her dismay, Sarah felt a hot rush of tears.

Nicholas finished the sentence while Sarah wiped her eyes on her sleeve. "He thought you'd only just left him. He thought you were still a little girl."

"After all these years!" said Mrs Askland. "And he's still..." She stopped in confusion. "Oh dear, I've never known how to put it, even to myself."

"*Alive*, we call it," said Nicholas. "Only he's not, just now. Ever since he thought he'd found you at that fancy dress party, but was mistaken, he's turned back into a toy."

"Oh," said Mrs Askland. "Poor, poor Drummond! I named him that, you know, after my father. But I still can't get over it. I've tried and tried over the years to work out just why Drummond Bear came alive when none of my other toys ever did."

"Oh, he told us how that happened," interrupted Nicholas, and repeated the explanation.

"I see," said the old lady quietly. "I suppose I *was* very lonely at that time. In fact, looking back, it would have been one of the worst times of my life if it hadn't been for that bear. But to think that he's still the same after all these years! Would you mind very much showing him to me now?"

Just at that moment, Kate burst into the room, holding a struggling bear.

Chapter 18

After All This Time...

KATE HAD been having a very exciting day. First a ride on a bus, then a walk through a lovely twisty garden with her mother, and then a nice plate of cakes and sandwiches as well. The only disappointment was the other teddy bears. None of them showed any signs of wanting to play with her as Drummond had done. And Drummond himself still wasn't talking. She couldn't understand it.

Another small annoyance was the way her mother kept stopping to talk to people. Kate didn't like it, so she tugged at her mother's hand and pointed to where Nicholas and Sarah were talking to Miss Honey and an old lady with white hair. "I want to go to Sarah!" she whined.

"All right, you go to Sarah," agreed Mrs Jordan, and went on talking.

Kate meant to go straight over to her sister and brother, but she thought she'd just have another look at the teddies on the big table first, and, while she was looking, Sarah and Nicholas went through a door with the other lady. Kate finished counting the teddies on the table. "Five, eight, two, three," she counted. "Look, Drummond. Five, eight, two, three teddies." But Drummond wouldn't look. It annoyed Kate, and she gave him a shake. "Sarah will make you look," she said, and trotted in through the same door that Sarah and Nicholas had gone through. She wandered past tables and chairs, and people turned to stare at her. Kate

didn't like it, but she knew her sister was there somewhere.

"I want Sarah," she said to a girl in a white apron.

"In there, pet!" the girl said, pointing through another door.

"I'm not a pet, I'm Kate," explained Kate indignantly. Several people began to laugh, so she turned and headed for the doorway.

"Sarah! Sarah! Where are you?" yelled Kate. She was only a little girl, but, like her brother, Kate had a very loud voice. Her sister did not answer, but someone else did.

"Sarah? Where is that girl?" called a muffled voice.

It was Drummond.

Kate stopped short. "Drummond, you've woken up at last!" she cried. "Sarah's in here." And she hugged Drummond as she marched into the office.

"Kate!" said Sarah.

"Drummond Bear!" said Mrs Askland.

Drummond turned puzzled eyes from one to another, and then began to struggle. Kate put him down and the bear waddled across the office floor, to stand gazing at the woman with the curling white hair and smiling blue eyes.

"Sarah?" whispered the bear. "*My* Sarah?"

They were interrupted once more just then by Mrs Jordan's worried voice calling out for Kate, and, shortly afterwards, their mother came in, all apologies and relief, and swept Kate out of the office. "Nick, your teacher's looking for you," she added.

Mrs Askland shook herself as if she had been asleep. "Could you tell her the children are with me and I'll bring them along in a few moments?" she asked.

Mrs Jordan nodded doubtfully and went out, with a protesting Kate in her arms.

Mrs Askland bent down and lifted Drummond onto the desk. "Well, Drummond Bear! After all this time!" she said. "I never thought I'd see you again!" There were tears in her eyes.

"Why did you leave me?" growled Drummond suddenly. "Tell me."

"It was all a horrible mistake, Drummond dear."

So Sarah Askland explained how it happened all those years ago.

"We got off the ship late one evening," she began. "And Father and I were taken to a boarding house for the night."

"In a car?" enquired Nicholas.

Mrs Askland shook her head. "There were very few cars at that time," she said. "Father was rather surprised that Uncle Jack wasn't there to meet our ship, but he must have decided to wait until the next day to find out what had happened. We were there for some days, as I recall, but while Father was still waiting for word from his brother Jack, I got sick with scarlet fever."

"What's that?" asked Nicholas.

"It was one of those sicknesses that no-one ever seems to get any more, like diphtheria and smallpox," explained Mrs Askland. "I remember we had just been to the dining room when I began to feel ill. I suppose a doctor was brought, and I was removed to the local cottage hospital. Most fever cases were nursed at home in those days, but, as we were in a strange place, and I had no mother, they must have decided it would be easier to take me away."

"But didn't you have Drummond with you?" asked Sarah. "When Nick had to go into hospital when he was little they let him take Tumbledown Ted."

Mrs Askland nodded. "Things have changed a great deal since I was a child," she observed. "People were afraid of scarlet fever, so any toys or clothes a person brought along to the hospital were usually burnt, in case of germs. So no doubt my father put you somewhere safe, Drummond, until I got better again."

"Just as well!" exclaimed Nick, and Sarah shuddered. "How awful if Drummond had been burnt up!"

"Of course I knew all along that, whoever was at fault, it could never have been *you*, my Sarah," said Drummond. "I never once wavered from that opinion."

Nicholas gasped aloud at this sweeping statement, and Sarah jabbed him sharply in the ribs.

"But *afterwards*," prompted the bear eagerly. "What happened afterwards? Not that *I* need any further convincing, of course, but I'm sure the children would like to know."

"Ah, yes, afterwards," said Mrs Askland regretfully. "Do you know, Drummond, I have never been at all sure just what did happen? I think my father must have contacted Uncle Jack during the time I was ill. I cannot now remember the reason why he wasn't there to meet us as arranged — possibly the ship arrived earlier than expected — but I do remember that I never went back to the boarding house. My father had all our baggage removed to Uncle Jack's house, and we followed as soon as I was released from hospital. It was a long journey in the train to get to my uncle's property, and it wasn't until some time after that I was able to be quite certain you hadn't been fetched with the rest of the baggage. How I cried about that! But my father was too busy to travel back to the boarding house and although I wrote a letter I never had a reply. To do my father justice, he did call at the boarding house the next time he made the journey, but by then it had new owners. I had always been afraid that some over-zealous person had ordered you to be destroyed in case you were harbouring any germs! It seemed only too likely . . . but now I know it didn't happen after all . . . thank goodness."

"Sarah! Nicholas! The school buses are ready!" called Miss Honey. "Come along now!"

The children got up hastily. Mrs Askland held out her hand to each of them in turn and held Drummond out to Sarah. "I'm so happy to have met you two," she said warmly. "You can't imagine what a relief it is to an old woman to have that ancient worry lifted after all these years. Goodbye to you too, Drummond Bear. Don't give these children too hard a time now, will you? And try to think kindly of me!"

The bear turned his head and stared from beneath the brim of his smart straw hat.

"What a lot of rubbish you do talk, my Sarah!" he said. "I'm not going with them. I'm staying here with you!"

Chapter 19

The Bear's Choice

KATE CRIED and cried when they told her that Drummond wasn't coming back. Mrs Jordan heard her and wanted to know what had happened. When it was explained, she was quite annoyed. "Even if it *was* her bear when she was a child, I'd have thought she'd have let you keep it now," she said. "I can't see how she can be so sure, anyway. There must be dozens of bears like that one about."

"No, there's only one Drummond," said Sarah. "She's even got a photograph and it's him all right, watch-chain and all. And she showed us inside the watch case where her initials are."

"*S.D.* Her name used to be Sarah Drummond," added Nicholas.

"Well, it just seems a bit mean to me," said Mrs Jordan, comforting Kate, whose sobs showed no sign of abating. "Never mind, Kate," she said cuddling her little daughter. "You still have Miss Prim to play with."

Fortunately Kate was too upset to retort that Miss Prim was not a real live toy, like Drummond was.

*   *   *

But Drummond was not happy.

And for some time he couldn't work out *why*. He had found his real Sarah, hadn't he? His one and only Sarah? So what more could a bear want?

Of course life with his Sarah wasn't the way he remembered it. On the ship she had had nothing else to do but play and talk with him. Now she had work to do in the Tearooms and office. And it wasn't as if he could roam about as he liked. There were customers and staff to avoid, and Mrs Askland's husband as well.

"Better not talk in front of John, Drummond Bear," said Mrs Askland with a smile. "The poor man might think he was going round the twist."

So Drummond spent more and more time hibernating, and each time his Sarah woke him he found it more and more difficult to remember who and what he was.

One morning he wouldn't stir at all. Mrs Askland shook her head. "Oh Drummond Bear, what are we doing to you?" she said aloud, and she put him gently on the office desk while she made some telephone calls.

After she had closed the Tearoom for the evening, she drove down the hill to Hawthorne and soon arrived outside the white house with a high green hedge. She knocked at the door and went in.

Sarah and Nicholas were waiting for her. Their mother had told them that Mrs Askland was coming for a visit, but they didn't know why. They hoped she would bring Drummond, but she seemed to be empty-handed. Mrs Jordan made a cup of tea, and she and Mrs Askland sat drinking it and talking about the Tea Gardens until Sarah and Nicholas were almost ready to burst with suspense.

At last Mrs Askland turned to them. "Would you two like to show me round your garden?" she asked.

Sarah and Nicholas exchanged glances and nodded. They had a feeling Mrs Askland didn't really want to see the garden, although she admired it politely enough, once they were outside.

"I would have loved that treehouse when I was a child," she said. "But I didn't come to talk about treehouses. I came to talk about Drummond."

"Yes? How is he?" asked Sarah.

"Not at all well, I'm afraid," said Mrs Askland gravely. "So I have brought him home to you."

"But . . . but it was *you* he wanted! He said so!"

Mrs Askland shook her head sadly. "It was *little* Sarah Drummond he wanted. The way I was then. Not the way I am now. I should never have taken him from you that day. So if you'll just come along to the car . . ."

Eagerly, they followed her and watched as she reached inside. "Here you are," she said, handing the lifeless bear over to Sarah.

"We'll bring him to visit you, won't we Nick?" said Sarah. They would have thanked Mrs Askland then, but there was a sudden pattering of feet and claws and Kate burst round the corner with Polly, the dog, capering behind her. She pulled up short and stared at the lifeless bear in Sarah's hands.

"Drummond!" she shrieked.

Drummond instantly stirred, sat up, and reached out his paws. Kate grabbed and hugged him . . . and his hat fell off.

"Oh dear," said her sister, expecting an angry lecture from Drummond.

"My Kate can do what she likes with my hat," announced the bear to the surprised children. "So long as she doesn't pull my nose off!"

"Can Drummond stay here now?" asked Kate, and Sarah Askland nodded.

"Good," said Kate, giving Drummond an extra hug.

"Goodbye Drummond Bear," said Mrs Askland, and held out her hand.

Drummond laid a paw in it. "I'll miss you, my Sarah," he said.

"I know, but not the way you missed these children," she answered. "You know, Drummond Bear, I have often heard people say how important it is for children to have teddy bears. What we all tend to forget is that bears need children just as much!"

She climbed into her car and drove away, leaving Drummond with Sarah, Nicholas and Kate.

"Let's go and tell Mum!" said Nicholas joyfully.

So they did.

But they didn't tell her everything . . .

The End

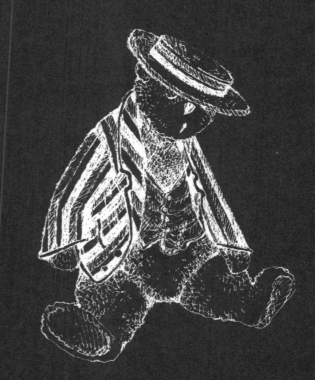